DISCREETLY
YOURS

by
Stephen Murray

Discreetly Yours

Copyright © 2019, Stephen Murray

ISBN: 978-0-9911940-3-2
$14.95us

Cover by: Jennifer Hart, harthousecreative.com
Formatting by: Self-Publishing Services,
selfpublishingservices.com

Other Works of Fiction by this Author
The Chapel of Eternal Love – Wedding Stories from Las
Vegas
www.thechapelofeternallove.com

Return to the Chapel of Eternal Love – Marriage Stories
from Las Vegas
www.thechapelofeternallove.com

Murder Aboard the Queen Elizabeth II
www.murderaboardtheqe2.com

Acknowledgements

To my family and friends –RJ, Sue and Maria and for all their support and encouragement.

To my writer's group – Sue, Gail, Nancy and Donelle for all their invaluable advice and suggestions throughout the process.

To Amy Al-Katib for her expert help with editing and for making the process a such an enjoyable experience.

To Michael Kimpel and Kristine Johnson.

To Jennifer Hart, harthousecreative.com, for her imaginative and creative cover design.

To James Kelly, Aspects of Writing and Brian Rouff, Imagine Communications.

My heartfelt gratitude to you all.

Table of Contents

PART 1
Frankie's Babes

CHAPTER 1

S atin turned off the Las Vegas Strip into the driveway of her favorite hotel, the opulent Bellagio, and steered her white Jaguar convertible into the valet parking area. It was twilight, her favorite time of day. The warm, gentle breeze flowed through her naturally blond, wavy hair. The famous dancing fountains were swaying back and forth to the same music she had heard so many times before. The wind blew a few light splashes of water across her face.

As she saw the parking attendant heading toward her, she wondered how many people across the world would give their eye teeth to be in her shoes right now.

"Good evening, Miss, and welcome to the Bellagio," said the valet cheerfully as he opened her car door.

"Thank you," Satin responded in her soft, demure voice as she moved her legs slowly to the side of the vehicle.

The eyes of the attendant widened as he watched this petite, thirty-something lady exit the vehicle, pulling her red dress down as she stood. He accidentally dropped the car receipt and stooped to rescue it before it could be blown away by a whiff of air. As he rose, he used the opportunity to stare at the curvaceous legs a little longer before resting his gaze on the upper half of her perfectly trim and stunning figure.

Satin felt his eyes stripping her naked as she made her way across the drive into the elegant hotel lobby, with its bold, imposing Chihuly glass ceiling.

She made her customary observations of the potential guests at the lengthy check-in lines. They always fascinated her. Where did they all come from? Why did they come to Las Vegas, specifically to the Bellagio? Were they gamblers? Tourists? Businessmen? Had they come here to get married? Or divorced? How many had come here to seek their fortunes? The expressions on their faces divulged nothing, but the assortment of people was as diverse as their heights, weights, and nationalities.

The pianist in the nearby cocktail lounge started to play the melodic "As Time Goes By." It was one of her all-time favorite tunes. She stood and listened for a few moments while looking at the observatory ahead of her. The theme of the atrium had changed since she was at the hotel the previous month. On her next visit, she would arrive earlier to wander through and marvel at the exquisite display. The gardens, though fleeting, were always so spectacular and unique.

Heading for the ladies' room, she checked her makeup and fluffed her hair. She pursed her lips and checked her lip gloss. After spraying a few drops of *eau de cologne* around her neck and hair, Satin ventured back into the casino.

"*Rien ne va plus*," came a voice from the roulette table.

The sound of the little ball spinning around the wheel drew her toward the only empty seat remaining. The ball rhythmically started to slow down and finally came to rest.

"Black 13," called the croupier as he raked in the chips from around the table. A couple of the female players squealed with delight as they saw their stacks of chips increase for being fortunate enough in having selected the winning number, or at least the right color. Simultaneously, there was a roar in the background. The familiar sound of coins crashing against a metal tray indicated that a lucky slot player had won a jackpot. The clattering sound seemed to continue for an eternity.

The gentleman seated next to Satin eyed her up and down. "Say, lady, you look like one classy broad. Can I buy you a drink?" he hollered while blowing his cigar smoke toward her.

She observed him with disdain. *What a crude and vulgar jackass,* she thought, as her eyes scanned this obese man in his bright yellow shorts, trashy sandals and obnoxious Hawaiian shirt. "No, you may certainly not!" she snapped tersely. *How dare he!*

"Sorry, lady. I thought ..."

"And so you should." She glowered at him, not wanting him to press further with any conversation. Unsure of whether or not the clod would accept her abrupt response, she moved to a nearby table and opened her gold, sequined purse to retrieve a few chips for betting. It was more the vibrant sounds and continuous action that excited her about the casino, not so much the gambling. She stuck with the minimum bet, and placed one chip on red.

"Would you like a drink?" This time, the request was from an attractive cocktail waitress wearing a skimpy little outfit, sporting dangly, crystal earrings and an excessive amount of rouge, lipstick, and mascara.

"I'll take a Manhattan, please." Satin knew the bartenders at the Bellagio always mixed the drink to perfection, never forgetting the magic touch - a maraschino cherry garnish.

"Sure thing, Honey," the waitress smiled, as she continued her way around the rest of the table, checking the glasses of the other players.

The drink did not take long to arrive. Satin sipped it slowly, while playing every alternative spin at the table – winning some times and losing others. She reached break-even point and looked at her watch. It was time to go.

Picking up her purse from her lap, she headed through the casino, passing the many blackjack tables where the dealers were feverishly sliding cards from the dealing shoe to the players. The ominous silence that always appeared to surround the solemnity at the baccarat tables indicated she was nearing the elevators. She was alone as the elevator made its way to the 15th floor. She exited, headed along the corridor, and knocked on the door of the suite.

"Come in," yelled a voice from inside. "The door's ajar."

Satin pushed open the door and entered the living room area.

"I'll be out in a moment." The voice came from the bedroom.

There was a bottle of Dom Perignon chilling in the silver ice bucket alongside two Waterford crystal champagne flutes that adorned the coffee table. She smiled as she walked around it and headed toward the window. How she loved the view of the Strip at night. The vista of the fountains below, the Eiffel Tower at the Paris Hotel across the street, and the myriad of neon lights flashing and beckoning into the distance.

"Hello, my darling."

Satin turned to face the man. "Hello, Marvin. How was your trip?" She looked at the oily man in front of her in his silk dressing gown. *My God, he looks worse and worse every time I see him,* she thought. *How in the world did I get stuck with this revolting slime ball?*

"It was just fine. How have you been since I last saw you?" He headed toward her and kissed her gently on the cheek. As he put his arms around her, he started to slowly undo the zipper at the back of her dress.

"Now, Marvin. You know the rules." She stopped him by putting her hand behind her back.

"I'm sorry." He broke away, headed toward the champagne and popped the cork.

"No, I mean the house rules. You know," she said, slightly embarrassed. She never felt she should have to ask for the money.

"Oh! Of course. It's in the envelope on the nightstand." He started to pour the champagne as Satin walked into the bedroom. She opened the envelope, counted several hundred-dollar bills, and placed the money in her purse.

Marvin locked the door of the suite and took the tray of champagne into the bedroom.

Satin unzipped her own dress and let it fall to the floor. Marvin handed her a glass and clinked his, as if to toast.

"Here's to the first Monday of each month, when I come to Las Vegas. Here's to us, Honey."

"Here's to us," she murmured back, completely repulsed by the man in front of her.

CHAPTER 2

At the same time Satin was walking through the casino, her best friend, Ruby, was across town in the northern part of Las Vegas, tucking her two little girls into bed.

"You look so pretty, Mommy. Where are you going?" quizzed 5-year-old Maria.

"Mommy just has a business meeting, Sweetheart."

Gabby, who was a year younger than her sister, yawned as she snuggled up in the next bed.

"Will you be able to read us a bedtime story before you go, Mommy? Please," she begged.

"Yes. Please, Mommy. Oh, please," Maria pleaded, tugging at her mother's clothing.

"Auntie Margaret will read one to you, just as soon as she gets here."

Where is she anyway? She should have been here half an hour ago, Ruby wondered. Margaret was as dependable and solid as a rock. Ruby hoped her sister hadn't been in some sort of accident. A sense of relief flooded her mind, as she heard the sound of a car engine pull into the driveway of her plush townhouse.

"Here she comes. Now, you be good little girls tonight. Do you hear me?"

The girls nodded.

"I love you both," Ruby said as she leaned forward and kissed them on their foreheads.

"Love you too, Mommy," they responded in unison.

Ruby headed down the stairs and into the living room, as Margaret was entering the front door. She looked frazzled.

Margaret was not nearly as attractive as her older sister. Being diminutive accentuated her slightly plump and matronly figure, although in a pleasing and homely sort of a way. Even as they were growing up, it was always Ruby who was the center of attention — the gregarious one who had all the handsome boyfriends. Margaret had been shy, and content to remain in the background. But Margaret was the one blessed with the giving and loving heart. Her wonderful, caring husband worshiped the very ground she walked upon. Their deep love was mutual.

Margaret gave her sister a big hug. "So sorry I'm late. There was an accident on the freeway." Running her hand through her own windswept, tomboyish-styled hair, she placed her bag on the couch, headed to the kitchen, and poured herself a cup of coffee. Ruby always had a pot made for her when she arrived.

"Where are the girls?"

"I've just put them to bed. They want a bedtime story. Sorry, I promised you'd read them one. I don't have time."

Margaret shook her head sideways. "I do wish you would give up this crazy life of yours. I'm sure the girls would prefer you to read them a story at night, instead of me. I wish you would just get a regular job. Find yourself a decent husband, like everybody else — a nice father for the girls."

"Don't start, Margaret. Not tonight," Ruby warned. "I don't have the time or the inclination."

"It's just that I worry so much about you. You're in a dangerous business. You're stunning. Look at you — a fabulous face, wonderful jet-black hair, a beautiful suntan and a figure any model would envy. I should be so blessed. You could have any guy you want. You're a catch for any man."

"Yes, Margaret. That's exactly what I am — a catch. And I give a man what he wants; he just pays a bundle for it. And that's how I want it to stay."

"But what will happen to you in a few years' time, when your looks begin to fade?"

Ruby saw a look of genuine concern in her sister's face. "Margaret, you know how it was for us as kids. We were bounced from foster home to foster home, from school to school. I couldn't wait to get away from it all. We had a miserable childhood. I hated every minute of it, except for you. My girls will get the best. I'm going to see to it that they get everything we didn't. Maria and Gabby will have a safe and secure home, nice clothes, and everything they could ever want. I'll put them through the best of schools, so they can go to Ivy League universities. That's what my job will provide. I cannot depend on any man to do these things for me — nor will I. I've already had two trips down the aisle. I don't get child support from Maria and Gabby's bum of a father. I don't even know where in the hell he is! The second scumbag had such a wandering eye, I'm surprised he could even see straight. I'm glad they're gone from my life. I'll never trust another man. I have to make it happen on my own. And believe me, I will. I'm taking control, and I love it."

Maria appeared at the doorway, clutching her stuffed, pink rabbit. "I'm getting sleepy. So is Gabby. Is anyone going to read us a story?"

"Oh, Honey. I'll be right in," Margaret promised.

Maria turned and headed back upstairs to her bedroom.

Ruby picked up her purse. "How do I look, Margaret?" She smiled and adopted a striking pose.

Margaret looked admiringly at her sister's svelte figure which was highlighted by her tight-fitting black leather pants and low-cut, bright, purple top. She hugged her sister again.

"You look like a million bucks, as always. You'd better go, or you'll be late. I do worry about you, though."

"I know. And I love you for it. I won't be back too late, I promise."

"Where is it this time?"

"Oh, you know. This is my regular, weekly, boring night with my boring, old geezer — the divorced banking executive who lives at Spanish Trails. All he ever talks about is money. Money, money, money!" She started down the pathway to her car.

"That's right, I should have remembered. Well, at least he has lots of money — and from what you've said, a gorgeous home."

She watched Ruby start the car and speed down the street to the nearby freeway.

Margaret closed the front door and stared around the living room. She had to admit her sister had made it all on her own, and she hadn't done too badly for herself, either. The furniture in the living room was contemporary and elegant. Several bold and striking paintings adorned the walls.

Ruby certainly possesses an eye for art, she thought. Somehow, the taste in modern art did not seem to conflict with the antique *objets d'art* housed in the large display cabinet. *How eclectic everything looks,* she marveled.

Picking up her coffee, Margaret ascended the stairs. On her way to the girls' room, she passed Ruby's bedroom and saw the light shining from the walk-in closet. She went in and observed the packed room of assorted pantsuits, dresses, and evening gowns, many marked with the name of the most fashionable designers. Margaret shook her head. *Ruby could open her own clothing shop.*

She stopped for a minute, put down her coffee cup on the nearby dresser, held some of the clothes against her body, and looked admiringly at herself in the mirror. She smiled as she thought of all the spectacular places Ruby had probably worn some of the evening dresses, and how she herself would never be invited anywhere that would require such elegant attire.

What different paths our lives have taken us, and in such different circles we've moved.

"Auntie Margaret, when are you going to read us our story?" wailed Maria one more time.

"I'll be right there, Sweetie," Margaret yelled, as she snapped herself back to reality.

She picked up her coffee, switched off the light in the closet, and headed to the girls' room.

Both girls smiled and jumped up and down excitedly when Margaret appeared in the bedroom. She sipped her drink before putting it down on the nightstand between the beds and observed how Maria had been so sleepy earlier and how she had suddenly sprung to life. *Typical kids,* she thought.

"Come on, settle down, both of you," she admonished, giving them both a kiss. "Now, what do you want me to read to you?" She picked up the book of fairy tales.

"The one about the girl who goes to the prince's castle. The one with the two ugly sisters," yelled Gabby.

"You mean *Cinderella?*"

"Yes! Yes! That one!" both girls screamed and giggled.

"Shush now! Are you both comfortable?" Margaret asked.

The girls nodded.

"We love you, Auntie Margaret," Gabby said softly.

"I love you too."

The girls fell quiet.

"Now then, once upon a time..."

*****

Ruby's thoughts were far away from her two children, as she pulled up in front of her client's mansion. She may not have cared that much for her client, but she certainly loved his home with its palatial appearance.

Maybe one day, I'll be able to afford the same, so my girls and I can enjoy a real life of luxury.

Ruby looked at herself in the rearview mirror and fluffed her hair. She heaved a deep sigh, collected her purse, headed up the cobbled pathway, and pressed the doorbell.

CHAPTER 3

The tires on the Infiniti screeched as Goldie put her car into reverse and sped out of the parking lot of the Mandalay Bay hotel and onto the Strip. It was dark and, in her haste, she almost knocked over a couple of pedestrians on the sidewalk. She was furious. Her nimble fingers pressed the touchscreen on her console to make a call. She heard the clicking sound as it automatically dialed, and waited impatiently as it rang.

Frankie was watching a ballgame on the TV in the office at his home. He leaned forward to pick up the phone, threw his legs onto his desk, and crossed his ankles. *Time to get some new boots,* he thought, as he looked at the somewhat worn heels on his scuffed leather Lucchese boots.

"Hello," he said into the phone, extremely annoyed his game had been interrupted at such a critical point. The game was tied in the ninth inning with the bases loaded — two men on, two men out.

"You damn son of a bitch, Frankie," Goldie screamed through the phone.

He sat upright in his chair and leaned forward, puffing his cigar. "Hey, just remember who you're talking to little lady," he warned, adopting a forceful tone.

"You set me up with another damn loser! This one really slapped me around. My dress is even ripped."

"Did you get the money?"

"Did you hear what I said, you bastard? The jerk you set me up with slapped me around!" She started to cry.

"And if you don't shut up, I'll slap you around too. Did you get the damn money?" He was getting agitated.

"Of course, I got the money," she sniveled.

"Now then, why don't you just calm down? You can drop the money off on your way home, and we'll talk. OK?" His voice began to soften, but Goldie noticed the slightly menacing tone.

"I'm tired of always getting these losers, Frankie. How come Satin and Ruby never seem to get these freaks? I thought the three of us were your A team."

"Babe, you are part of my A team. You get these clients because you can handle them. Satin and Ruby have class. That's what their clients like. They pay for classy escorts. Yours like someone gutsy and feisty — a little trashy. That's what they pay for — trash. You know what I mean, Babe? There's a market for that."

"Don't be crass. I'm sick of you demeaning me. I'm done, Frankie."

"You'll be done when I say you're done and not a second before! Do you hear me?" the tone of his voice now angry and threatening.

Goldie was familiar with his mood swings and irrational behavior. She thought back to her 25th birthday party, where she had met him. After working for him for five years, she wondered whether it was bipolar disorder or the drugs that contributed to his unpredictable temperament. She remained quiet, hoping he would calm down.

Frankie took her silence as submissiveness. "Now, are you on your way over with the money?" he asked.

"I'll be there in five minutes to drop it off," she said softly.

"That's a good girl. When you get here, I'll have a little extra something for you for your troubles tonight. A little something you like inhaling from time to time." He knew too well of her cocaine addiction and had used it many times to his advantage — to make sure she would never be able to leave him.

Goldie hung up.

Frankie fumed that he had missed the end of his ballgame. *How dare she treat me like that?* He walked to the bar and poured himself a Jack Daniels on the rocks.

A few minutes later, the doorbell rang. Knowing it was Goldie, he put his drink down on the table. *I'll put that trash in her place if it's the last thing I do.*

Frankie opened the door to his palatial mansion, and Goldie stepped inside. He slammed the door and grabbed her by her flaming-red hair. She stumbled as he pulled her along the hallway.

"Ouch! Stop it, Frankie! You're hurting me," she yelled, her voice filled with pain. But her plea fell on deaf ears. "Please, Frankie," she begged. "I'm hurting. What did I do?"

She tried to pummel him, but she was no match. His 6-foot-2-inch body overpowered her diminutive 5-foot-4-inch frame. He stopped in front of the full-length mirror at the end of the hallway, still holding her hair.

"Just remember who's the boss around here," he snarled as they both looked at each other's reflections.

How she loathed and despised the curly haired, paunchy bloodsucker with his pockmarked face. She hated the gold earring dangling from his right ear and his gold necklaces that nestled in his gray, hairy chest.

"Yeah, well you just remember who has paid for this mansion," she gesticulated, her hand waving abstractly at the cathedral ceilings, the extravagant staircase, and the ostentatious furniture. His home was like a royal palace and reeked of opulence, albeit many of the furnishings she considered kitsch.

He slapped her across the face and held her hair firmly, pointing her again at the mirror. She shrieked from the pain.

"Now you listen to me, and you listen good," he threatened. "I run the most exclusive escort agency in Las

Vegas. And you could have had this too. Instead, you chose to spend your share of the pie on this, didn't you?" From his pocket, he pulled out a small plastic bag filled with white powder and teasingly waved it just out of her reach. She tried to grab it, but it was not within her reach.

"And look at where it has got you," he continued. "Look at yourself."

Goldie looked at herself in the mirror and at the ripped, black velvet dress. Her tanned face was hardened and lined through years of sunbathing, and the drug usage had clearly taken its toll on her once smooth skin. *Perhaps I haven't taken care of myself, but my figure's still in good shape.*

"You're a fiery redhead. You've got a lot of spunk, and you seem to satisfy your customers. I run the best operation in Vegas and take care of you well. No one will ever treat you like I do," Frankie sneered.

They paused as they looked in the mirror, each summing the other one up. After an awkward pause, Goldie spoke. "Will you buy me a new dress, since this one was damaged?" she asked wistfully, almost plaintively.

"Sure, I will, Babe," he said gently, as he slowly ran his fingers through her hair. "But don't you ever tell me you're done," he yelled and pulled her hair back. "Do you get me?" he asked, gripping her hair back even tighter.

Goldie nodded. They stood, momentarily quiet.

"Can I have some of that stuff, Frankie?" she asked meekly and with a degree of trepidation.

He let go of her, snatched the small, black, sequined purse she'd been holding and took the hundred-dollar bills from inside.

"Please, Frankie, may I have some of that coke?" she begged.

"That's better," he teased. "See how nice I can be when you talk to me right?" He pulled out of his jacket pocket a smaller plastic bag than the one he originally showed her and placed it in her hand.

"This isn't what you showed me earlier." She was annoyed and frustrated.

"But there's plenty more where it came from. You know I'll share it with you."

He took her by the arm, led her back along the corridor to the front door, and showed her out. "Now you just run along, and get a good night's sleep. Remember your tomorrow morning regular when Francoise gets off his night shift."

"I hate you, Frankie," Goldie responded with sheer venom in her voice.

Frankie laughed loudly at her and slammed the door shut.

CHAPTER 4

Frankie returned to his TV to watch the analysis of the baseball game. *Damn! Looks like I missed the end of a good one. To hell with that bitch.* The phone rang. It was Satin. "Hi, Babe. How did it go?"

"Same as usual. You know what a slob he is. I wish I didn't have to see that creep. If it's OK with you, I'll bring in the money tomorrow, after my appointment with Roy." Last names were never mentioned over the phone, and it was one of the rules she had never broken.

"Sure, Babe. You can bring the cash in when you're ready. We can arrange for someone else to see your 'creep' as you call him, in the future."

Satin's radar went into full alert. It was not like Frankie to be so nice. What was his motive? Frankie was never this accommodating unless it suited him. She waited to see if he had anything else to say.

"Are you still there, Babe? Can you hear me?"

"I hear you, Frankie."

"Good. By the way, you'll not be seeing Roy tomorrow. I've arranged for you to see someone else."

Satin didn't like the direction the conversation was headed. "Why won't I be seeing Roy?"

"I thought I would add a touch of variety to his life. You know what I mean?"

"Roy has always been one of my best clients. He pays top dollar every time. I thought you promised him your number one, Frankie. That's me." Satin had always been confident. Yet, for the first time, she was unnerved.

"I know. But I've arranged for Pearl to see him tomorrow."

"Pearl? You mean that new hussy who recently came onboard?" She was dumbfounded.

"Yeah! You know the one. She's young and spunky."

Satin was now indignant. "Roy has always been more than happy with my services. There's no way Pearl can compete with me."

"That's where you're wrong, Babe. From what I've heard, she's showing a lot of promise. She's bringing a lot of repeat business. Let's give her a break and see what happens. We can also give her your 'slob' or 'creep' or whatever you call him, since you're not satisfied with him."

Now, Satin fully understood his game plan — he was slowly cutting her loose. Frankie wouldn't be able to get rid of her that easily, though. She just needed a little time to think about what course of action to take.

"Have it your way, Frankie," she said tersely, but coolly. "Who do I see tomorrow?"

"Let me call you later, Babe. There's someone at the front door." He hung up, and made his way along the corridor. He was not overly surprised to find Ruby on the other side. "And how's my favorite little treasure? Was it still good with Daddy Warbucks, the banker, tonight?" Frankie asked, beckoning her into his home with a gesture of his hand.

"Cut the crap, Frankie. Here's the money." She handed him the stack of one-hundred-dollar bills as she stood in the doorway, waiting for him to split the cash.

"No need to rush. Come on in, Babe, and have a drink. We have some business to discuss."

"It can't take long, Frankie. I have to be home."

Ruby walked into the living room and ensconced herself in the large leather chair. She looked disgustedly at the ashtray on the glass coffee table packed with cigar butts and ash. *Hmmm, Goldie's just been here,* she thought, as the aroma of Goldie's cheap perfume still permeated the air. It didn't mingle too well with the smell of stale cigar smoke.

"That's right, you have two little kids waiting for you, don't you, Babe? I'm sure they miss their mummy at night." He mixed her a vodka and tonic, placed it on a plastic coaster sporting a deck of cards, and set it on the glass table in front of her.

Ruby ignored the drink, as she did his question about the children. She ran her fingers through her hair. "What is it you want to discuss, Frankie?" she asked directly.

"Hey, Babe! No need to rush. Sit back and relax. Can't you just enjoy a drink with Frankie?" He shrugged and mixed himself another drink. Ruby eyed him suspiciously. She hated it when he called her babe. He called all the ladies babe. She wondered if the rest of them disliked the label as much as she did.

"No, I'm tired and I want to go home."

"Sure." He counted the money and handed her the cash.

She flicked through the notes, adding the amounts on the bills in her head. She recounted. "Frankie, you've shorted me a hundred bucks."

"No, I didn't, Babe. That's the business I wanted to discuss," he said. His voice was mocking and contemptuous. "You and me, Babe. We're going for a new split." He sat next to her and patted her on the knee with his hand, holding his glass in the other.

"I don't think so, Frankie," Ruby shot back defiantly, shoving his hand away from her knee. "Give me my hundred bucks," she demanded.

Frankie became belligerent. "I don't think you heard me, Babe. You have in your hand all you're going to get. Now, you don't want to make Frankie angry, do you?" he snarled, the tone laced with sarcasm.

"That's not right, and it's not fair, Frankie. You know it's not." Ruby was now more upset than annoyed.

Frankie jumped up from his seat and pointed his finger in her face. "Don't you dare tell me what's fair and what isn't!" he yelled. "I'll determine what's fair."

Ruby stood up to leave. "You're not the only game in town, Frankie." She headed down the hallway. Frankie followed her. As she opened the front door, he grabbed her arm.

"Neither are you, Babe. Neither are you. But don't you think of leaving me. You don't want anything to happen to those little girls of yours, do you?" he sneered.

Ruby was shocked. She looked him directly in the eyes. "Don't try to intimidate me, Frankie. And don't you dare touch or go near my girls, or I'll kill you," she threatened, her fiery temper rising. She could see the hatred in his face. Never had she known such a despicable person. *I can't believe this bastard is in my life.*

Frankie grabbed her arm forcibly. "Just remember who you're talking to and who calls the shots around here - Me. Not you. Now, why don't you just run along home and take care of those little girls of yours? Make sure you're at your appointment tomorrow." He glowered at her.

Ruby returned the stare for a moment, as a silence fell between them. She glanced down at his hand that was still clutching her arm. "Let go of my arm!" she ordered. Frankie let it go, pushing her away.

Ruby hastened to her car and drove off. When she was out of Frankie's sight, her eyes welled with tears. Frankie's attitude weighed heavily on her mind. As she visualized her two precious little girls, the more enraged — and frightened — she became at Frankie's apparent threats. The car seemed to drive on autopilot, while Ruby pondered her situation. There was an internal desire to keep driving around instead of going home, so she could clear her mind. But she knew too well that Margaret was expecting her and would be anxious were she not home soon. *What a love. I'm truly blessed to have such a sister.*

It was not long before she pulled into her driveway. Margaret peered through the curtains. Ruby smiled. *So typical. Such a worry-wart.*

Margaret turned on the outside light and embraced her sister as she walked through the front door. "Is everything alright?" she asked with her customary tone of anxiety, which reflected in her face.

"Everything's fine, just fine," Ruby said as she threw herself onto the sofa, setting her purse down next to her, and kicking her shoes off. She was not of a mind to divulge her conversation with Frankie. Margaret would panic, and certainly wouldn't understand the occupational hazards of the job. "How were the girls?"

"No problem. They never are. I had barely started their bedtime story when they both fell fast asleep" Margaret laughed softly. "Can I pour you a drink or make you some coffee?"

Ruby shook her head. "No thanks." She really wanted to be alone. "There's no need for you to stay, Margaret. I know you have a hubby at home and work tomorrow."

"Ok, Sweetie." Margaret gathered her sweater and purse and kissed her sister on the forehead. "Nighty-night. I'll call you tomorrow." She opened the front door.

"Margaret," Ruby called.

Margaret turned around. "Yes?"

"I love you. And thanks."

"Love you too," Margaret said with a smile and closed the door behind her.

Ruby reflected in the quiet of the room — everything seemed so still. She pulled her phone from her purse and sent a text message to Satin. *Can we talk?*

The response was almost immediate. *Not now. How about at the gala party?*

Ruby was confused and quickly typed back: *What gala party?*

The charity fundraiser this Friday night. I'm sure Frankie asked you. Over and out.

"Damn! I forgot about that. What will I wear?" Ruby said aloud. She sent a text to Goldie and waited for a while to see if there was any response. After a few minutes, she gave up. *Probably stoned,* she thought. She switched on the TV and flicked through the channels to see if there was something worth watching. Unable to find anything, she turned it off, grabbed her purse, and headed upstairs to bed. She switched the light on at the foot of the stairs while turning off the neighboring switch, putting the living room into darkness. At the top of the stairs, she looked into the girls' bedroom. They were both sleeping so peacefully. "I love you, my little angels," she whispered softly. She continued along the hall and walked into her bathroom. After she removed her makeup and undressed, she climbed into bed.

Frankie better not dream of touching my girls. I'll see him dead first she thought, as she tossed and turned, desperately trying to fall asleep.

CHAPTER 5

Satin was looking at herself in the vanity mirror as she was attaching her false eyelashes. Having a hunch that Pearl would be in attendance, she was determined to look her best at the gala party that evening. From her earlier conversation with Frankie, it was obvious the new kid on the block was destined to take her place. *Over my dead body,* she thought as she finished applying her makeup. She stood up and looked at herself admiringly. *We'll see who's No. 1.* She smiled and winked at herself, switched off the lights, set the alarm, and headed for her car. *I wonder what it is that Ruby wants to discuss with me.* She recalled the sense of urgency in Ruby's text message two nights prior. *Couldn't be that important, otherwise she'd have called me yesterday,* she rationalized. *Maybe it's time for a wig meeting.*

A wig meeting was when Satin, Ruby, and Goldie met with each other. They all wore wigs as disguises, so they could meet incognito, and they always arranged to have lunch at different restaurants in numerous casinos on the Strip — the ones that were less frequented by locals, especially on the weekends. That way, the likelihood of them being recognized was minimized. Each of them parked their cars on different levels of the garage, so there would be no obvious trace of their meeting.

The drive to the party was not long, and Satin soon pulled up in front of the valet. She took the elevator to the penthouse and quickly surveyed the crowd as the doors parted.

Now this is classy. When she was told it was to be a star-studded gala to raise funds for the homeless, she knew it would be her kind of party. She loved events where men were clad in tuxedos, sporting black ties, and the women were all dressed in elegant evening attire. There were normally a couple of clods who never fully read the 'formal attire' section on the invite and stood out like sore thumbs. It was pleasing that no one had fallen short at this affair, as everyone seemed to be dressed appropriately. How she hated the casual, open-neck, short-sleeved-shirt type of gatherings. This was much more her style.

Satin entered the room and immediately took a glass of champagne off the tray as the waiter passed by. She hummed to herself, in tune with the combo playing soft jazz in the far corner. It was barely audible over the chatter and laughter of the hundred or so guests in the large room.

She stood for a while, surveying the scene in front of her, feeling the ambience. The floor-to-ceiling windows round the outskirts created a magnificent panoramic view.

She marveled at the flood of lights flickering for miles on the houses below, and the thousands of stars twinkling in the sky over the penthouse suites of the myriad of hotels. *What a perfectly beautiful and romantic setting.*

Satin recognized a few of the male guests but gave no hint of acknowledgement. She could not see Ruby or Goldie anywhere. Suddenly, she spotted Frankie in another corner talking to Pearl. She wondered whether she should go and speak to them, before thinking better of it.

"Can I interest you in a canapé?" inquired the server.

Satin looked at the silver tray with its colorful array of appetizers.

"We're offering petit phyllo cups with baby rock shrimp on a bed of dill pesto," he said with a French accent.

I hope that's not all I am offered this evening. Satin smiled to herself and then at the server. "Not at the moment, thank you. They do look delicious and tempting though."

Now, completely absorbed in the atmosphere and fully comfortable with her surroundings, she strolled through the room, trying to locate Ruby. She finally eyed her walking toward the powder room and immediately headed in the same direction.

"Oh, thank God, you're here." Ruby seemed relieved as she saw Satin's reflection in the mirror.

"Everything OK?"

"Has Frankie approached you about changing the split in money? He dropped that bombshell on me the night I texted you. I was wondering if he's changing your split."

Satin shook her head.

"What do you think his game is?" Ruby was mystified.

"I don't know, but I don't like it. When I spoke to him last, he wanted to replace one of my best clients."

"Who?" Ruby asked, stunned.

"Someone I have been dealing with for years. He sent Pearl last week."

"Pearl? Are you kidding?" Ruby turned to face Satin. "She's way too inexperienced and far too young."

The reference to age struck Satin cruelly. She gave a wan smile. The door to the powder room opened, and a middle-aged lady entered.

"Excuse me," the woman smiled, as she sat in front of the mirror and started busying herself with the contents of her purse. "Heavenly party, isn't it? And my, don't the two of you look stunning? Just love those earrings," she said to Ruby. There was a southern drawl to the intruder's voice.

Ruby and Satin looked at each other, knowing they wouldn't be able to continue their conversation.

"Thank you," Ruby said and smiled. "Yes, the party's divine."

The lady pulled a lipstick from her purse as Satin and Ruby left the room.

Satin observed Frankie striding across the floor toward them. "Here comes Frankie," she warned. "We'd better separate."

"I'll go talk to Goldie," Ruby quietly mumbled.

"I think it's time for a wig meeting. Maybe tomorrow, lunch time. The place we planned the last time we met."

"I was thinking the same thing as I was driving here tonight. Tomorrow it is." Ruby headed off, leaving Satin to deal with Frankie.

Satin was aware of the look Frankie had on his face and knew he was not happy. She didn't care. One of her strengths was being able to maintain her composure, which she knew irritated him. It would do so this time.

"What the hell do you think you are up to?" he muttered through his gritted teeth.

"Why Frankie, surely you don't begrudge a girl a visit to the powder room, do you?" she smiled.

"I begrudge you not working on my dime."

"I'm not on your dime, Frankie. Just remember how you make your money. It's not from you working yourself into the ground."

"Don't push it, Satin."

"Oh, knock it off, Frankie," she scolded. "Stop messing with my client base, and we'll continue to be just fine."

He started to respond, but before he could get a word out, she interrupted. "Now, if you'll excuse me, I see a mighty fine-looking gentleman at the bar."

She headed toward the distinguished-looking, silver-haired gentleman, who she immediately recognized. She crossed paths with the waiter again and grabbed another glass of champagne from the tray just before taking the vacant seat at the bar.

The gentleman eyed her up and down and smiled. Satin sipped her champagne and put on her most seductive look. She sensed he was nervous.

"Lovely party, isn't it?" he asked.

"Delightful, and for such a good cause," Satin responded.

"My name's Roger."

"No, it's not, Judge. I know better than that," she teased. "And what does it say of a system when you have a judge who lies?" she continued, wagging her finger at him.

The gentleman blushed and looked embarrassed.

"Hmm," he coughed. "OK. Then you know it's Richard. Have you appeared before me at some time?"

"Now, Judge. Why would a nice lady like me appear before you?" she taunted, enjoying the game she was playing.

"Well, how else would you know me? We've never met before, have we?"

Satin sensed his apparent discomfort and the awkward manner he was displaying.

"Who hasn't seen your strong, handsome, debonair, face? It was plastered on all the billboards throughout the city when you ran for election."

"Oh, of course! It seems so long ago now — I almost forgot. How stupid of me." He chuckled uneasily. "I didn't catch your name."

"That's because I didn't tell you," she toyed. "It's Satin."

"Ah, now *you're* not being truthful." He smiled at her, beginning to relax.

"But I don't have to be; I'm not a judge. Besides, what's sauce for the goose is certainly sauce for the gander," she quipped.

"Touché!"

There was a brief silence as he looked down at his glass and played with his drink. The ice cubes rattled against each other. The band switched the tempo from its peppy beat to a slow, quiet tune. The female singer started to croon the torch ballad with her soft, velvety voice.

"Would you like to dance with me?" Satin asked.

He shrugged. "Not sure if that's such a good idea. A man in my position seen dancing with a stunningly beautiful woman like yourself. What would my wife say?"

"And just where is your wife?"

"Back east, visiting my daughter at college." He started into a discourse about his daughter, which Satin did not want to hear. She cut him off, deciding to opt for the bold approach.

"Well, since your wife is having a good time with your daughter, maybe we could dance in your hotel room? No one would see us there," Satin challenged.

He thought for a moment. "What makes you think I have a hotel room?"

Satin smiled. "Now Judge, don't insult my intelligence. By evening's end, you'll have consumed more than a couple of drinks, and you don't want your name splashed all over the headlines of tomorrow's newspaper, do you?"

They stared at each other. He was seduced by her beauty, candor, and charm. She was attracted to his power, not to mention his devastatingly good looks.

"See you in room 705 in 15 minutes." He rose from his seat and left.

Satin sipped her drink and looked at the mirror in front of her, noticing Frankie's glowering look in its reflection.

CHAPTER 6

The gala party was in full swing. Ruby observed the gentleman with whom Satin was conversing, leave the bar, and she wondered what happened that prompted Satin to remain behind. Ruby, not one to pay too much attention to current affairs, did not recognize the judge as Satin had. She had been trying to locate Goldie when she finally saw her bouncing around on the dance floor. The challenge was how to attract Goldie's attention.

She smiled and was envious. *If there is one thing Goldie knows how to do, it's dance. What rhythm and movement she has.* She looked at Goldie's dance partner and immediately felt sympathetic. He was obese, and sporting a poor-fitting tuxedo. The bright red cummerbund looked as if it were ready to pop off his portly stomach. Sweat was pouring from his face, and he looked awkward trying to groove to the sounds of the combo — his hands flailing in the air. *Poor Goldie. She always seems to attract the losers. This one is clearly no exception.* Ruby was unusually oblivious to the gentleman standing alongside her as she tapped her feet and swayed slightly to the music.

"Excuse me," he said, as he gently touched her arm. "Looks like you would prefer to be out there with them. Would you like to dance?"

Ruby turned to face the gentleman whose deep voice had sounded so sexy in her ear. He was impeccably groomed, with penetrating dark eyes, silver hair, and a grin that displayed a dashing set of white teeth.

I can't believe my good fortune. Not only do I get to dance with this hunk, but I get the opportunity to talk to Goldie without getting Frankie rattled. Ruby knew Frankie watched all his girls like a hawk at these types of functions.

"I'd love to," she replied, reaching out to take his hand as she led the way to the dance floor. She positioned herself next to Goldie and started to move in time to the disco beat, hoping that the next number would be a slow ballad, where she could snuggle up close to this man and place her hands around his neck. She started to turn her body around in time with the music, allowing her partner to see her entire package and found herself facing Goldie. "Wig meeting tomorrow at noon," she mouthed slowly.

Goldie indicated she understood the message by swaying her hips, and hoisting her two thumbs in the air. The message delivered, Ruby turned to face her partner.

The music stopped, and the tempo changed to a slow song. Ruby was disappointed that her partner took her right hand with his left and placed his right hand around the small of her back. It was the formal dance position, which was not what she was hoping for. *Guess I'll have to work a little harder tonight,* she mused.

There was a brief silence before he entered into a conversation.

"And what brings a beautiful lady like you to a fundraising function alone?" he whispered.

My God, this man can whisper all the sweet nothings he wants into my ear. I have never known such a sexy voice. "How do you know I'm alone?" she asked in a demure voice.

"I didn't until you just told me," he smiled.

Their eyes met, and she returned his smile.

"But I'm glad you are," he continued. "Alone, that is. I am too."

"Good. I'd hate to be taking you away from your date or your wife."

"Ah! Now you're fishing," he teased. "But don't worry, little lady. I have neither."

"The name's Ruby."

"What?" He sounded confused.

"You called me little lady. My name is Ruby."

"Of course," he laughed awkwardly. "Sorry. My name's Shane."

"And where are you from, Mr. Shane?"

"No, Shane's my first name. I'm from Oregon — just here for the fundraiser. And you?"

"Oh, I live right here in Las Vegas."

The music ended, and the beat changed to a tango.

Shane grimaced. "Can we sit this one out? Tango is not my forte."

"Sure we can. It's not my favorite either."

They left the dance floor. Ruby noticed how Goldie was stuck doing the tango with her partner, who clearly did not understand the rhythm and was totally unaware of how embarrassing he looked. She was thankful she was with Shane — at least for the moment.

Frankie was eyeing his girls and was pleased with what promised to be a good night's haul. Ruby's catch, judging by the debonair appearance, was extremely affluent. He looked at Goldie struggling to do the tango with her partner. He chuckled. *Boy, what she won't do for a snort.* Even so, he was astute enough to know that the guy she managed to hook had money — and plenty of it. His appearance and behavior were so gauche, it had to be his money that granted him access to such an event. He looked back to where Satin was seated and was troubled by the departure of her male companion. They seemed to be making contact. Frankie knew the man's face, but couldn't quite place it. But the fact that Satin was still sitting at the bar, not making any moves, indicated she had the situation under control — unless she was just waiting for someone else to approach her. *She couldn't have let such a good catch get away, could she?*

He cast his eyes around the room to see where Pearl was. *Like flies around a jar of honey,* he smiled, observing the many men surrounding his latest find. Pearl was thriving on the attention of the group gathered around her. *This one will be a real gold mine,* Frankie thought. *I'll have to remind her the evening is not about her — it's about landing a guy. She needs to learn how to nail one down quicker and not stand there, basking in her own glory.* Nonetheless, he considered his good fortune and lit up a cigar.

The tango was getting to be too much for Goldie. "Harvey, can we skip this and get a drink? I'm thirsty." She removed his clammy, roving hand from her derriere and placed it higher around her waist.

"Sure, Honey." He smiled and led her from the dance floor toward the bar.

Goldie squirmed as she felt his fat, sausage fingers grabbing her hand. *What a creep,* she thought. *How do I always end up with these weasels? Frankie better not shortchange me on the stuff this time. I have no idea what this freak will want from me.*

Satin was still at the bar. She saw Goldie and Harvey walking in her direction. Aware that Frankie was still watching, she did not want to be seen sitting next to Goldie, knowing he would go on one of his rampages about his girls fraternizing at events. She didn't think he would ever learn — they seldom acknowledged each other at these functions, except in the restrooms. She looked at her watch. *Thank goodness, it's time me to leave, anyway.* She finished her drink, nodded and smiled at the bartender, and left. Frankie was pleased. As he saw Satin leave the main entrance, he surmised she had plans to meet her 'companion' at an agreed time in a different location. *Darn. Where do I know his face from?* Frankie was desperately trying to think before the vision faded from his mind.

Pearl excused herself from her group of admirers and headed toward the restroom. Frankie rose from his seat and blocked her path.

"Pardon me, Frankie. I need to go to the powder room."

"I've been watching you, Babe. By this time of the evening, you should have already picked your mate." He exhaled the smoke from his cigar and blew it right in her face. Pearl grimaced, as she fanned the smoke away.

"But Frankie, I thought you'd be proud of me. Look at all the potential clients I'm lining up. They're all smitten with me." Pearl adopted a tone of mock petulance.

"Not smitten with you, Babe. Smitten with what they can get from you."

"It's all the same to me, Frankie." She side-stepped him and continued to the powder room. As she passed, he grabbed her arm. "Remember, Babe, I make the rules." She winced as he tightened his grip. "Please let go, Frankie. You're hurting me."

"Don't forget who runs the show."

Pearl shook her head. "Of course not."

"And you will learn how it is done." He motioned in the directions of both Goldie and Ruby.

Both of them were standing up, had their escorts in tow, and were moving toward the exit. Pearl nodded gently and eyed Frankie suspiciously.

He winked and let go of her arm.

CHAPTER 7

Ruby looked at her watch. It was 1.00 a.m. As much as she enjoyed Shane and his luxurious hotel suite, his time was up. She rose and started to dress in order to be home before the girls woke up. *Where would I be without Margaret?* she thought.

"Must you go?" Shane asked from the bed.

"Yes," she responded flatly. "I gave you your options at the beginning."

He rolled onto his side, watching her tighten the zipper on the back of her dress. He suddenly cast his eyes downward, his one hand playing idly with the duvet. "I wasn't completely honest with you, Ruby." He paused to see if there was any reaction.

"Oh?" She was noncommittal.

"Like I said, I'm from Oregon and here for the fundraiser, but that is only a part of it. I'm also in Las Vegas looking at houses. My company is transferring me here, and they suggested I spend some time during this visit looking for a new home."

"Why are you telling me this now?" She started straightening her hair in the mirror. Inexplicably, Ruby was miffed by his deception. She was accustomed to being lied to by her male clients — it was an unspoken part of the job — but she disliked Shane's sudden candor and the discomfort she felt. She didn't want to hear his confession.

"Well, I was hoping you would come and help me look at properties. I don't know a soul in this city. I also hope I'll be able to see you again."

She turned to face him. "Looking at homes isn't quite my scene, Shane. I don't think I can help you. Besides, you wouldn't want to pay my rate just to look at homes when there are realtors who would help you for free … would you?"

Shane looked forlorn. "Well, I was kind of hoping you would just do it as a friend."

"A friend? Shane, we hardly know one another."

"We've been to bed together," he responded.

"That was a business deal. Strictly business."

"You're not going to tell me you didn't enjoy it, are you?"

"You don't get it, do you? You paid for a service, which I provided."

Shane seemed genuinely crestfallen. "Are you trying to tell me we can't be friends?"

Ruby turned back to the mirror. "Rule number one in my line of work is to never mix business with pleasure," she stated, somewhat coldly and very matter-of-factly.

Her daughters were her life now. They were her prime consideration. There was no time for romantic dalliances. That was how she wanted it and how she liked it. She could see his face in the mirror and noted the dejected look. *Boy, this guy sure is one sad puppy.* She suddenly felt some empathy for him and decided to change the direction of the conversation. "When will you actually be moving here?"

"It's supposed to be in two weeks, but the company will put me up in a hotel for a month if I haven't found anywhere to stay."

"Are you looking forward to living in Vegas?"

He shrugged, still toying with the blanket. "It will be nice to have a fresh start. After my divorce, things have been hard. A clean break might be good for my ex and me. At least there are no kids to worry about." He paused for a moment then continued, "You don't have any kids, do you?"

Ruby shot him a glance while collecting her purse.

"Oh, that's right. I'm sorry. You told me last night you didn't have any kids," he said.

Ruby suddenly felt a pang of guilt for being annoyed with Shane over his deception. She certainly had not been candid about her own past. She didn't know why but, impulsively, she opened her purse and handed him a card. "If you really need help looking for a place, I'll give you a hand. I'll also give you a discount, but I can't do it for free. As I said, business is business."

He looked at her card and then back at her. "You mean, this is it?"

She nodded and smiled, then left the room.

✳✳✳✳✳

Across town, Goldie was bidding farewell to Harvey.

"Well, Harvey, your time is up, and I have to run. Where's my cash for the extra hour?" She waited while he reached for his wallet. *I wonder why I always get the tightwads.* She pondered that thought as she looked around the sparsely decorated motel room, with its drab, faded drapes and carpets covered with cigarette burns and stains. Even the clock radio on the bedside table seemed antiquated, with its useless red numbers that did nothing but flash obnoxiously. She found the musty odor repugnant. *Why do Satin and Ruby always get the guys with the classy hotel suites, and I always get stuck in these hellholes?*

Nonetheless, she had to admit that even though her clients were cheap when it came to accommodations, they were pretty generous when it came to paying for her services. Harvey turned out to be no exception, and she was elated when she saw how much he handed her.

"You did good, Honey. Can I call you?" She flicked through the notes and stuffed them down her tight-fitting top. "You sure can, Mister. Here's my number." She smiled as she handed him her card and leaned forward to give him a kiss on his forehead, making sure he had a full view of her cleavage.

Harvey smiled back and watched her head toward the door. She turned to give him one last seductive look. She looked at his portly paunch protruding like an anthill beneath the sheet. *What a loveable creep — he's one of the least demanding clients I've ever had.* "Next time we rendezvous, just make sure you have plenty more of the good stuff," she teased.

"Are you talking about my sexual prowess or the powder you seem to be so fond of?" he joked.

"Maybe both. What do *you* think?" she taunted seductively and closed the door behind her.

Once in her car, she retrieved the cash and recounted to see if she summed it right from her initial observation. Though it was dark, she was able to see the numbers on the bills with the help of the dimly lit 'no vacancy' sign, despite its missing letter 'y.'

Wow! This guy really is something else. Easiest money I've made in a long time. And he even threw in a couple of lines for me to snort. What a trip! And what a kick! I think I can turn him into a regular. I hope so.

She lit a cigarette, started the car, and turned on the radio. She was completely exhausted and couldn't wait to get home and put in a good few hours' sleep before the wig meeting. *I wonder what prompted this meeting.* The thought dominated her mind as she hurried along the freeway. She recalled how Frankie had treated her the last time they met. *What a louse! What a total bastard!* She wondered if Ruby and Satin were also being treated this way. *Don't know what has gotten into him! But one thing's for sure: I'm not going to take any more lip from him. The next time will definitely be the last time.* She flicked her cigarette ash into the ashtray and opened the sunroof. *Hopefully, the night air will keep me awake.*

The harvest moon was shining brightly, and the sky was full of twinkling stars. There was barely a cloud in sight. The freeway was surprisingly void of traffic in both directions. Goldie turned up the volume on the radio. Tammy Wynette's recognizable rendition of "Stand by Your Man," with its twangy guitar, played loudly through the car speakers.

"All very well for you to say, Tammy. You have a man to stand by," Goldie said aloud. "Some of us don't have that luxury. And at this stage of my life, I don't even know if I want it anymore."

She flicked the cigarette butt out the window and sang along with the lyrics as she pushed her foot a little harder on the accelerator and sped home.

*****

It was early in the morning, and Richard was lying in bed in his hotel suite, with one hand propping his head up on the pillow and the other holding a cigarette. He had a slight headache from drinking too much at the party the previous evening. But what a night it had been, and what a satisfying sexual partner Satin was for him.

Satin was fully clothed and sitting on the side of the bed, slipping on her high heels. She looked through the small opening of the drapes, where the bright rays of sunshine beamed through. The tile roofs of the concrete buildings and houses that seemed to stretch as far as the eye could see were only curtailed by the mountains in the distance.

She stood up, moved closer to the window and stared out. *My God, how I loathe this city during the day. It must be the drabbest city in the world.* She looked at all the hotels along the Strip and pondered the millions of secrets that were kept by the walls of those rooms. *If only they could talk.*

The sound of Richard's voice snapped her back to reality. "A penny for your thoughts?" he asked.

She did not care to share them. "Will I see you again?" she asked in a soft and hesitant voice. She, too, had enjoyed their shared intimacy and harmonious lovemaking. There was something different about this man.

Richard shifted uncomfortably in the bed and snuffed out his cigarette. "Well, I don't know about that. It's difficult for me. You see…."

Satin braced herself and didn't allow him to finish the sentence. She threw her hands in the air. "Oh, I know you have a wife to consider and — don't tell me — a position to think of."

"Now Honey, you understand, I'm sure." He climbed out of bed and moved toward her, starting to massage her shoulders while tenderly caressing her cheeks with his masculine lips, reliving the way they touched each other a few hours earlier.

She didn't understand. She never had. But she was accustomed to the line. "You win some, you lose some," she responded nonchalantly, trying to sound indifferent even though she was aching for his touch. "But you will have to see me one more time at least."

"Oh?" Richard was taken aback and removed his hands from her shoulders.

Satin turned to face him, appreciating his virile and hairy chest. She looked him in the eye. "One small item you seem to have overlooked. As a judge, certainly you will not want to pay me with a traceable credit card, and I am sure you don't have the required amount of cash with you."

Even though her own personal rule was to always get the money upfront, Satin knew the judge would not want to use a credit card. She trusted him to come through with the cash, since she knew he wanted to keep his infidelity private.

Richard was embarrassed and uncomfortable. He turned and scratched his head. "You're right. I don't have the cash. This is the first time I've done this. I've always been faithful to …."

Satin cut him off again. "Save it, Judge. I don't want to hear how you love your wife and kids." She reached into her purse and pulled out one of her cards. "I know you're good for it. I expect to hear from you later." She handed him the card and headed for the door.

"Wait, Satin. Please. Wait a minute."

Suddenly, his cellphone rang, startling him. He answered to hear his wife's voice.

"Hi, Darling. Thank goodness you're all right. I tried calling you at home, but you're obviously not there. Where are you so bright and early?"

"Oh, I had a couple of drinks last night and stayed at the hotel." He turned away from Satin, embarrassed by the phone call.

"That's right. The fundraiser for the homeless. How was it? Did you have a good time? Did you see anyone we know?"

"No. I didn't stay for long. It was quite boring and uneventful," he lied.

Satin had been in this situation so many times, but she was not prepared to listen to the same lies she had heard countless times before. *Just like all the rest of them,* she thought.

"What do you and Deidre plan on doing today?" asked Richard, deftly changing the subject.

"Oh, women's stuff. We went shopping for clothes this morning. We're about to have lunch, and we're treating ourselves to a facial this afternoon."

"You mean I'll be treating you to a facial this afternoon."

"Can't you come and join us, Darling? It's an easy flight from Las Vegas. Deidre would so enjoy it."

"We've been through all that, Honey. You know my caseload at the court. Please, let's not go over that again."

Satin detected that he used the same term of endearment for his wife as he had for her.

"You're right. We'll talk later. Love you, Darling."

"Love you too."

Satin stared at him. He looked sheepish.

Shrugging at her, he said, "You know how it is."

"No, I really don't know," she responded.

"Can't you stay and talk?"

"About what? Deidre's grades? I don't think so. Is this why you wanted me to wait a minute? To listen to you and your wife?"

Ignoring her questions, Richard looked at the card in his hand and sat on the bed thinking of the previous night. *Wow, what a night of passion. I've never made love like that before. But God, what if it ever comes to light? Can Satin be trusted?* He then thought about his wife and child and the phone call. Pangs of guilt overcame him. He leaned forward and buried his head in his hands, swallowing hard. It was the first time he had ever betrayed his marriage vows. Now, he would have to carry this burden of guilt forever. He felt so alone … and empty.

Satin headed to the door and turned. She put her hand to her lips, blew him a kiss, and winked. "It was great while it lasted, Honey." She used the term sarcastically. "I know I'll hear from you soon."

She left.

CHAPTER 8

atin looked at her watch. It was noon. She scoured the restaurant to see if Ruby or Goldie had arrived, already knowing she would be the first one there — she always was. Ruby arrived late for every wig meeting, invariably with a feeble explanation about the babysitter being delayed. Goldie was normally the last to arrive, offering the usual lame excuse for her tardiness - she "overslept." Satin always chalked it up to the fact that Goldie had to make the long journey back to Earth after her drug-related highs sent her into outer space, but she kept her thoughts to herself. It was her hope that neither of them would be too late. She was not in the mood for any nonsense.

"Party of one, Madam?" inquired the hostess breezily.

"Actually, a party of three," responded Satin. "We'd prefer a booth if possible."

"Not a problem. Please step this way."

Satin followed the hostess to a nice, relatively secluded booth toward the rear of the restaurant and seated herself where she could view her two friends when they arrived. Much to her surprise, Ruby and Goldie appeared five minutes later. She waved to them and obviously caught Ruby's eye as they moved in her direction. They all embraced and sat down.

"How are the girls?" asked Satin.

"Oh, they're fine, thanks. Maria is getting more adult every day and really looks after Gabby. Margaret was late getting to the house today, that's why I'm a bit late."

"And I overslept," added Goldie.

Satin rolled her eyes as she looked at her two best friends.

"You know, it is one thing that we all wear wigs to these meetings, but I do wonder whether it is necessary for us all to wear dark glasses," Satin proclaimed. "I feel like a female member of the Mafia."

"Well, it does help conceal our identity, which is the general idea," countered Goldie. "It's never bothered you before."

"No, Goldie. The idea is to be unobtrusive. All of us wearing the glasses make us conspicuous."

"Well, if anyone should remove them, it should be you, Satin," Ruby chimed in. "With that wig and those glasses, you look like Jackie Onassis, for God's sake. That automatically makes people notice you."

"If it comes to that, maybe you could take yours off," retorted Satin. "That way, with your hairdo, you don't look quite so Audrey Hepburn. It's not as if we are having *Breakfast at Tiffany's*."

"Why don't we just take them off?" Goldie suggested calmly. "We so seldom get together, is this really the purpose of our wig meeting today?" She stopped as she saw the waiter coming toward the table.

"My name is Ramon, and I will be taking care of you today. Can I interest you ladies in a cocktail before lunch?" he asked as he laid the menus on the table.

"Make mine a cosmopolitan," said Satin, removing her sunglasses.

"And for you, Ma'am?" Ramon asked, looking at Ruby.

"Grey Goose Vodka and tonic for me, please," Ruby responded, stuffing her glasses in her purse.

"Make that two," added Goldie.

As soon as Ramon departed, she tucked her glasses on her blouse and continued. "Hey girls, I know we normally don't discuss our clients, but I couldn't help but notice yours last night, Ruby. He sure was a hunk. Yours had his back to me, Satin, so I couldn't see him. How did you both make out? Did you just meet them there, or are they regulars?"

Satin shrugged. "Mine was a local guy. He just got carried away in the moment. He felt guilty this morning and started to unload on me. I felt like charging him extra. Hell, psychologists charge a bundle just for listening."

Ruby understood. "Yeah, but that comes with the territory, Satin. You've been around long enough to know that."

Satin winced. "I know, but even so, there was something about him. I feel there is more to this guy than the one-night stand. We'll see. I don't want anything to materialize on a regular basis if he has all this guilt every time."

"Mine was a novice and a liar," Ruby said, matter-of-factly. "Not a novice in bed, mind you, but a novice when it comes to sleeping with ladies like us. He's here from Oregon and will be moving to Las Vegas. After the roll in the hay, he expected me to go looking for houses with him, like we are the best of buddies. Can you imagine?" She stopped as Ramon arrived with the drinks.

"Have you decided on your lunch selections, ladies?" he asked, order form and pen in hand.

They didn't need to look at the menus. Ramon wrote the order for three chilled melon soups, two crab salads, and one shrimp salad, and then he departed.

"Well, mine was kind of a creep," divulged Goldie, not allowing Ruby to finish her story. "But he paid well and was easy to please. He likes to have a snort too, and he shared some with me," she giggled.

"I do wish you'd get off that stuff, Goldie. Why don't you go to Narcanon or something like that?" pleaded Satin. "We worry about you." She put her hand over Goldie's.

"Oh, that's sweet of you." Goldie felt embarrassed. "You needn't worry about me. I'm fine. I'll always be fine. Harvey — that's the guy I met last night — I think he will become another regular. Sure, I don't get to stay in the fancy hotels like you two, but he sure paid me the big bucks, like all my other clients."

Satin cast her mind back to her judge. She hoped he would come through with the money. Her hunches told her he would. He would not be able to handle the threat of a scandal, and obviously his wife and daughter meant a lot to him. *At least Goldie's clients always seem to know what they want, and they pay her for it,* she thought.

"Satin's right," Ruby said with conviction. "We do worry about you."

"I think we should all worry about Frankie," Goldie retorted. "He's been getting on my nerves lately. The clients he's been hooking me up with have been pretty rough. I could strangle him."

Ruby and Satin exchanged glances. This was the first time Goldie had ever mentioned anything about the treatment she was getting from her clients. They both had inklings, having seen her covered in bruises at previous wig meetings, but never before had Goldie actually raised it as an issue.

Satin wondered if Frankie was playing games with Goldie the same way he was with her. "I think our 'caretaker' is jerking us around, and I don't like it," she said. "We're supposed to be his A- team. He's started taking away my top clients and giving them to Pearl. You been noticing anything strange, Ruby?"

"Are you kidding? This week, he changed my take on the action, and then he threatened my two girls if I did anything. I told him I'd kill him if he even touched them."

The conversation ceased as Ramon arrived at the table with the chilled melon soups. Once he was out of earshot, Ruby continued. "I'm serious," she said. "I wouldn't think twice about it."

"Well, that's if I don't get to him first," said Goldie. "I really am at the end of my tether with that louse. Problem is, where would we go? What would happen to us?"

Ruby was dismissive. "He's not the only game in town. I told him that. That's when he started his threats."

"He isn't the only game in town, Ruby. You're right. But he does have the market cornered when it comes to 'who's who' in the world. Let's face it. We've all done well by Frankie," said Satin, savoring the soup.

"And he's done well by us," countered Goldie. "We can all see what's happening. It looks like we're all getting the shaft from this bastard. What do we do about it?"

Ruby finished her drink. "I've already told you. If he so much as goes anywhere near my girls, I will kill him. Sorry ladies, I know that would force you to look elsewhere for work, but we're talking about self-preservation here. My girls are my life. This job isn't."

"Not necessarily, Ruby." Satin's mind started going into top gear. "If Frankie were to disappear from the scene, we could run the business. We're all familiar with where he keeps the records of his clients. We could contact them all, discreetly remind them of who we are, and inform them we are now running the show. I'm sure none of them would dare go elsewhere. We could all make a fortune."

"Well, it would probably help put Maria and Gabby through college." Ruby laughed and appeared nonchalant, without giving Satin's proposal any serious consideration.

"It would be worth it to me just to be rid of Frankie," said Goldie. "I'd do the deed, if I could be certain to get away with it. Any ideas?"

Having finished her soup, Ruby placed the spoon in the bowl. "My God. You guys are serious, aren't you?"

A silence befell the table as the three women exchanged looks and contemplated the ramifications of their discussion.

Ramon appeared at the table, removed the soup bowls, and replaced them with the salads. "*Bon Appetit*," he said.

"Can I get you anything else? Another round of drinks, perhaps?"

"Another round of drinks will be just fine, thank you," said Satin. "Just fine."

CHAPTER 9

The restaurant started to fill up, and their booth was no longer isolated.

"Methinks this is a grave situation that needs to be explored more fully," said Ruby.

Satin and Goldie fully understood the code word. Whenever one of them used the word 'grave,' it meant the need for the conversation to be private. It was a way of communicating to meet at the cemetery immediately following their current rendezvous. They were not likely to be seen or heard there.

"Agreed," Satin and Goldie responded in unison.

Ramon returned with the drinks, and the ladies continued to savor their salads. The conversation for the duration of their lunch was as stilted as it was muted. Normally, the conversation between them flowed, as they would chat about all and sundry. Yet, today was different, as they wondered what was going through each of their minds. Was it trepidation? Anxiety? Nervousness? Fear? Guilt?

The usual indulgence of dessert was skipped, and they settled their own checks with Ramon. As was the custom after the wig meetings, Goldie would visit the restroom, Ruby would stop at one of the stores in the hotel, and Satin would head straight to the parking lot. By staggering their exits, they were less likely to be seen together.

Naturally, Satin was the first to arrive at the cemetery and pulled up under the tree nearest to the fourth bench. She tapped her fingers on the wheel in time to the music that was playing softly on the radio and watched the proceedings of the funeral service taking place much further down the graveyard. After what seemed an eternity, Ruby and Goldie's cars appeared in her rearview mirror.

Ruby emerged from the car, clutching a small bouquet of red roses with a smattering of baby's breath and green foliage, all neatly wrapped in cellophane. The three made their way to the bench in the shade, and Ruby placed the flowers on the grave in front of her. "I think we should rotate the buying the flowers from now on," she said. "I know I've always done it in the past when we have our meetings here."

"Well, you were always the paranoid one who insisted we bring flowers to place on the grave of someone we don't even know," Goldie shot back.

"I just thought it made our being here more credible, less suspicious, that's all," Ruby retorted.

Goldie lit a cigarette. "Yeah … right. And how would it look if some of the deceased's family showed up? How would we explain the flowers to them?"

"Knock it off, ladies," Satin interjected. "We have more pressing things to worry about. Are we going through with this idea or not?"

There was silence as they each waited for the others to speak first. The atmosphere was quiet and serene. Birds could be heard chirping over the muffled sound of the traffic that surrounded the cemetery gates.

Finally, Ruby spoke. "I'm all for it. I was OK with Frankie and thought I could deal with him. But once he raised the subject of my girls and threatened them, he crossed the line."

"Do you think he was serious?" asked Satin.

Ruby turned and looked at her. "That's a gamble I'm not prepared to take. I'm in."

Goldie flicked the ash off her cigarette. "As I mentioned at lunch, I'll be happy to be the one to do the deed. The sick leeches he's sent me to see lately, they're the scum of the earth. I get knocked around by the clients, and then when I see Frankie, he knocks me around too. I've had it. I couldn't see a way out. Now I do." She hesitated, before adding, "As long as we're in this together."

"Like the three musketeers," Satin mused. "One for all, and all for one. How ironic."

"But none of us have sufficient business knowledge to run the operation," said Goldie.

"Nonsense. You could oversee Frankie's girls, Ruby could handle the finances and bookkeeping, and I would handle the clients," suggested Satin.

"Hey, makes sense. Works for me," said Ruby, knowing the business relationship would be just as cordial as their friendship had been. "Question is, how do we get the deed done?"

"Well, I have a gun," said Goldie.

Ruby was stunned. "You're kidding?"

"What's the big deal? I've had it for years."

Ruby shook her head. "I just never figured you as a gun owner."

"Well, you've obviously never had to deal with the kind of clients that Frankie sends to me."

Ruby suddenly felt sorry for her friend.

Satin's mind was already racing. "You know what, ladies? This brilliant idea is just coming through my mind. The Fourth of July is coming up — it's on a Sunday this year. You can both come over to my place, and I'll barbecue. We'll have drinks on the porch beforehand. You know my nosy neighbors — they will be peering out the window as they always do, and they'll provide the alibi for all of us. You can park your car in front of the house, Goldie."

"I don't see where this is going," said Goldie.

Satin was getting excited as the scheme was unfolding in her mind. "My neighbors on the other side, the Moyles, always go away for Fourth of July weekend. They give me the keys to their house and the garage opener."

"I'm with Goldie," Ruby said as she scratched her forehead. "You've lost me."

"It's a snap," said Satin. "Ruby, the night before, you bring your car over and park it in the Moyle's garage. As you know, all the garages on our street are in the back and face out into the alley. I'll run you home. On the actual day, Goldie, you can pick Ruby up. That way, you'll both be seen arriving at my house together. We can be out in the front for quite a while as you pretend to admire my beautifully pruned rose bushes and the flowers in bloom. That will give us enough time to be seen by the neighbors. We'll have drinks on the porch and, after a while, we'll make our way around to the rear patio. I'll heat up the grill and put on some noisy music. The two of you can slip out the back and head down to Frankie's office. You can circle the block, Ruby, while Goldie does the deed. Since it's a holiday, the office complex will be empty. You can be there and back within half an hour. While you're gone, I'll have the hamburgers cooking. When you arrive back, slip into the Moyle's garage again, and sneak in through the back garden. Then, we'll take the food to the front porch to eat in full view of the neighbors."

Ruby and Goldie sat and thought through Satin's plan.

"What if Frankie doesn't go to his office that day?" questioned Ruby.

"He always goes to the office on holidays," said Goldie. "He always has, and he always will. He never has anywhere else to go."

"You need to make sure you retrieve his rolodex of clients," said Satin.

"And remove any records he has of us," added Ruby.

Goldie lit another cigarette. "All sounds too good to be true. Let's all sleep on it and think it through. We can meet here the same time next week."

Satin's phone rang. "I'll bring the roses," she said as a nod to Ruby, while she rummaged through her purse for the phone. As soon as she answered it, she recognized the voice and rose to walk away from the bench. Her voice was soft and alluring. "Why, hello. What a pleasant surprise."

"This is Richard. Judge Richard ..."

Satin cut him off. "Yes, I know who it is. What can I do for you? Do you have something for me?"

"Yes, can you meet me in half an hour at Barnes & Noble on West Charleston, across from Boca Park?"

"Sure, I can be there in 30 minutes," she replied.

"I'll be in the science-fiction section, browsing through the books," he said as he hung up.

Satin smiled. *We may just have an extra, unplanned insurance policy,* she thought. "Gotta go, ladies. Until next week. We can work out the finer details then."

Goldie picked up the roses from the grave and handed them to Ruby. "Since there is nobody around to see, you might as well take these flowers home for yourself."

They returned to their cars and just managed to turn them around and head for the exit before the funeral cortège formed at the end of the cemetery.

CHAPTER 10

Satin's car pulled into the parking lot of Barnes & Noble. She removed her wig, ran her fingers through her hair, and, using the rearview mirror, refreshed her lipstick. *I wonder if Richard has arrived yet.* Once inside the store, she picked up a shopping basket and, as directed, made her way to the science-fiction section, where she observed her one-night stand nervously turning the pages of a book. She sauntered alongside him, said nothing, and casually viewed the books on the rack, ignoring both the titles and the authors. Science-fiction had never been her favorite genre. *This could very well be some scene straight out of a science-fiction novel itself,* she mused. The electricity between them was tangible to her, as she recalled the excitement of the previous evening.

Slowly turning his head, Richard made sure there was no one in sight. Out of the corner of her eye, Satin watched him remove an envelope from inside his jacket pocket and place it inside the novel he was holding. She raised her arm, holding her shopping basket, cluing Richard to deposit the book there. She waited a while to see if he would say something, but sensed his discomfort. He removed another book from the rack, accidentally dropping it to the floor. As he stooped to gather it up, she removed the envelope from the book in her basket, folded it and placed it in her blouse pocket, leaving the book in the basket. *This could be some good insurance. The book has to have the Judge's fingerprints all over it. Who knows how long he'd been playing with the book before he placed the envelope inside?* As Richard stood up, she whispered to him in quiet tones, as if in a library. "I'll take that," she said and held the basket out. Without a word, he dropped the second book in the basket. Satin turned and made her way to the checkout counter. "I'd like both of these, thank you," she said to the assistant, placing the shopping basket on the counter. "No, I am not a member, and I'm not interested in becoming one."

Leaving the books in the basket, the young, male clerk scanned them. Satin handed him the cash. "No need for a bag, thank you," she said, gingerly picking up both books between two fingers. *I can't believe my good fortune. I now have extra insurance. Who knows if it will be needed, but it certainly can't hurt.* She left the store.

When she got in her car, her phone rang. She was surprised upon seeing Richard's telephone number — she made a mental note of it when he called her at the cemetery. She resisted the impulse to answer the phone, deciding instead to let it go to voicemail.

During the drive home, Satin anguished over Richard. *He's perfect. Almost too perfect. Yet, he's happily married. But not so happy if he can fool around — even if it was the first time. Who knows if it even was the first time? Just because he said it was, doesn't make it so. He lied to his wife; he could just as easily lie to me. But what a lover. I bet I brought out the best in him, too.*

She pressed the garage opener in her car and pulled inside. *Goodness, I've driven all the way home on autopilot. I hate that.* She opened the door to the house, removed a bottle of wine from the fridge, and poured herself a glass. *What a day it's been. I'm exhausted.* She sat down on the couch, kicked her shoes off, and put her feet on the coffee table. *Never mind Richard. I have more important things to deal with. I wonder if Goldie and Ruby will have cold feet when we meet next week.* She became so engrossed in thought, she totally forgot to play back Richard's message.

*****

Ruby stopped in her driveway. She removed her wig and wrapped it in tissue paper before placing it in the Nordstrom's bag, which was always used to house it. She ran a brush through her hair and heard her two daughters yelling.

"Mommy! Mommy! You're home."

Ruby opened the car door to greet them, hugging them both. She saw the sweetness and innocence in their eyes. She felt a sense of relief knowing that she didn't have to worry about anyone harming her two little angels, if the plan was implemented.

Margaret appeared at the front door. "Hi. Do you want coffee or a glass of wine?"

"Wine would be great, thanks. Pour yourself one too."

"I don't have time, unfortunately."

"Come see what we did today, Mommy," said Gabby as she tugged at her mother's hand.

"Give me a few minutes, Sweetie. Your Auntie Margaret has to leave, and I need to talk to her. Both of you run along upstairs. I'll be there shortly."

The girls ran upstairs, laughing and chatting incessantly to each other as they went.

"I know you've invited us to your Fourth of July barbecue this year. But could you take care of the girls for me that day?" Ruby took a sip of the wine Margaret had poured, as she sat on the sofa,. massaging her aching feet. She immediately saw the frown appear on her sister's face.

"Ruby, you know it's become a tradition at our house. It'll be the usual gang that always attends."

"I know. It's a lot to ask. You'll have your hands full with all the food preparations and so on. It's always so spectacular. There's just something I need to do that day."

Margaret sat beside her and reached out for her hand. "What is it, Ruby? Something's troubling you. I know it is. I haven't been your sister all these years without learning when things aren't right."

Ruby looked at her sister, wondering how much, if anything, she should divulge. *Best to say nothing at this point in time. Not sure yet if Goldie will go through with it. If she changes her mind, as much as I'd like to see Frankie dead, I'm still not sure I have the guts to pull the trigger.*

*****

Neither Ruby nor Satin needed to wonder whether Goldie had second thoughts. Goldie left the cemetery feeling grateful there was a plan to get rid of Frankie. Even though she would be the one committing the crime, it was comforting that Satin and Ruby were complicit. Between them, they would come up with a truly fool-proof plan. *Frankie has abused me for the last time,* she thought. *Boy, going into a partnership with Ruby and Satin ... we can have a great future together. God, I'm so lucky to have such good friends.*

"Shut up!" she yelled out loud to the driver behind her who was honking his horn. She hadn't realized the traffic lights had changed to green. Her foot moved from the brake to the accelerator, and the car sped off.

The car phone rang. It was Harvey, her 'date' from the night before.

"Hi Gorgeous, how about a repeat of last night?" he asked.

Wow, that's sweet. It's been a long time since I've actually been called gorgeous. She had to think quickly. *I don't know. He **is** weird.*

"Well, Gorgeous, do you want to, or don't you?"

"Where and when?"

"What about eight o'clock? We can meet for dinner at Martha's Deli."

Jeez, the last of the big spenders for sure. Well, at least he pays me well. I suppose I'd rather have the cash than have him splash out on a gourmet meal and a plush hotel. I could use the money. "Make it eight-thirty," she said. "I'm on my way home, and I need to freshen up."

"Good deal," Harvey said. "See you then, Gorgeous."

Goldie smiled, accelerated faster, and cast her mind back to the wig meeting at the cemetery. She suddenly felt the urge to call Satin.

"Hi, Goldie." Satin feared that Goldie had changed her mind already.

"Satin, I just wanted you to know, I'm not backing out of this. You can count on me. I'm glad we're in this together. You know what I mean?"

Satin smiled. "As I said, Goldie, All for one, and one for all."

"I just had more questions, but I guess they'll have to wait until next week. It's too bad you had to leave so abruptly."

Satin suddenly remembered she had not played back Richard's message and brought the conversation with Goldie to a close.

Realizing the books were still on the passenger car seat, she grabbed some paper towel and a large zip-lock bag from the kitchen and hurried to the garage. She retrieved the books with the paper towel, touching the same spots she did when she held them at the book store. The books, along with the receipt, were placed in the zip-lock bag and secured in her small safe.

Satin returned to the couch, drank some more wine, tucked her feet underneath her, opened the envelope from her blouse pocket, and counted the bills. She was overjoyed — and somewhat surprised — at how much he had paid in excess of what they had discussed. She played back the message from Richard.

"Hope you are happy, Satin, and that I can count on you. Perhaps we can meet again. I'll call later." The click of the disconnect was abrupt.

Just what the hell is that supposed to mean? Satin frowned. She was irritated. *Hopes he can count on me? For what?* She was of a mind to call him back but decided better of it. *Do I want to try and cultivate this, in case I need him later? Or do I remain detached? I probably already have enough insurance from him. But then again, one can never have too much.*

Surprisingly, he had her in a quandary. She had always been able to keep her clients compartmentalized — separate from her social life. Richard was different though. Satin could tell she would have to grapple with her feelings for him — more than she already was.

CHAPTER 11

Doesn't seem like a week since I was here, thought Satin, as she parked her convertible in the cemetery. She was pleased to see Ruby and Goldie had already arrived. *That's one for the books.* Roses in hand, she made her way through the headstones to the bench where they were seated. "Here are your stupid roses, Ruby," she said, handing them to her friend.

"Thanks, Satin. Boy, these are beautiful. Much better than the ones I always get. Where did you buy them?" Ruby inspected the perfectly-shaped buds.

Exasperated, Goldie shook her head. "Damn it! Who cares about the darn flowers? Is that why we're here today? To discuss roses?" She threw her hands up in the air and rolled her eyes.

"A little testy, are we? Having second thoughts?" Satin asked. She sat next to Goldie, while Ruby placed the flowers at the graveside, peeling off the few dry petals.

"Hell, no!" Goldie removed her sunglasses to reveal a deeply bruised eye. "This is from Frankie. There was a mix up over a client this week. I know it was his mistake, but he swears it was mine. This is what I got for arguing with him," she divulged, pointing to her eye. "I was ready to shoot him right then and there."

Satin squeezed Goldie's hand tightly. She felt for her friend who was being treated so badly. "I'm convinced our plan will work," she assured the others. "We just need to refine a few details."

Ruby joined her fellow conspirators on the bench, putting her arm around Goldie, gently patting her shoulder. "Details?" she asked. "I thought the plan was solid."

"It is," replied Satin. "But we need to zero in on some specifics, like clothes. Goldie, you will need to bring a change of clothes to my house, so you can change before you go to Frankie's. If you are spotted, you can't risk being recognized in anything from your existing wardrobe. And if you buy something new, they can trace the purchase. Ruby, perhaps you can find an old blouse or sweater you haven't worn in ages. Bring it with you when you come over with the car the night before. I've got an old wig I haven't touched for at least ten years. She can wear that."

"Oh, great," said Goldie. "Some fashion statement I'll be making."

Satin turned and stared at her. "Goldie, you're going to kill a man. You're not modeling for the cover of *Vogue* magazine. We just don't want you to be recognized, that's all. It's a precaution. You need to be inconspicuous."

"So you're having me dress like some old-fashioned broad? Won't that make me stand out even more?"

"Satin's right, Goldie," interjected Ruby. "Don't worry. I'll give you one of the old silk tops I purchased in Hong Kong years ago. They're plain and timeless. And, you know how wigs are — you can simply restyle to suit you."

"Well, be sure and have the wig ready for me to play with when we arrive. I don't want to go into Frankie's building looking like a derelict."

"In a silk blouse?" asked Satin. "I don't think that's likely to happen. Be sure you bring something you're willing to part with, Ruby. As soon as Goldie gets back, that top becomes evidence, and we're going to burn it. We'll toss it in the barbecue after we're done eating. I'll cut up the wig and dispose of it in various trash bins along the Strip.

I'm assuming you'll just be wearing regular denims when you come here, right?"

Both Goldie and Ruby nodded.

"Another thing," she continued. "You'll need to leave your cellphones here when you drive to Frankie's."

"Why?" asked Goldie.

"You should know. With technology these days, they can track where you are any time of the day or night by the location of your cellphone and whether you answer it," said Ruby.

Goldie lit a cigarette. "OK. If that's the case, then how do I let Ruby know when I'm ready to be picked up?"

"Ruby will drive around the block for about five minutes before parking in the lot across the street. She'll have a clear shot of Frankie's office window from that spot. Switch the lights on and off two times when you're ready to leave. By the time you get to the parking lot, Ruby will be there."

"Hey," said Ruby. "I'm not sure I want my car sitting in a parking lot, with my license plate in full view, broadcasting to the world where I am."

"Don't worry. I've thought of that," Satin said without an ounce of uncertainty. "Last week, I went to the movies. It was dark when I came out, and as I headed to the car, I tripped over a license plate in the parking lot. I was wearing open-toed shoes, and the sharp edge cut my big toe. I picked it up and tossed it in my trunk, so no one else would get hurt. Must be divine intervention. I was planning on throwing it away as soon as I got home, but for some reason, I never got around to it. I guess God does work in mysterious ways."

Goldie flicked the ash off her cigarette. "You're a genius, Satin. You really have thought of everything. But my gun is a Colt 45. Even shooting through a cushion, it may still make a muffled sound."

Ruby was stunned.

"Well, why doesn't the gun doesn't have a silencer?"

"Oh, they don't make them for Colt 45's, Ruby. Hey, it's not as if I go around shooting people every day. I'm not a real expert, you know."

"No need to be sarcastic, Goldie," said Satin. "We just want to make sure you're covered. Even if the gun does sound loud, it's the Fourth of July. Fireworks are going off all over the place. You can never tell which direction they're coming from. Frankie always has his TV blaring at a deafening pitch. He told me once that on Independence Day, he likes to watch the fireworks from Washington, D.C., on his big-screen TV. They always go off at the same time as they are playing Tchaikovsky's 1812 overture, with all the canon and mortar effects. Your gunshot will sound just like one of the fireworks. Besides, who's going to hear it, anyway? Frankie will probably be the only one working that day. Everyone has somewhere to go on the Fourth of July. Everyone, of course, except patriotic Frankie."

They all laughed.

Goldie was the first to turn somber. "Seriously though, what if I'm caught? What if I'm identified? What if I do have to stand trial? I don't want a public defender. What chance would I stand? I don't have the money for an attorney." She cast her eyes downward, embarrassed. "You know where my money goes."

"You get rid of that habit," said Ruby, "and I'll help you out. My Daddy Warbucks, as Frankie calls him, is my weekly regular. He's a bank president. Lives in Spanish Trails. Just loaded with dough."

"But you need him as a client." Goldie stomped out her cigarette and immediately lit another one. "I can't let you lose a client."

Satin smiled. "You still don't get it, do you Goldie? After this we won't be worrying about clients. We'll be getting all the clients from Frankie's entire business. We'll be raking it in."

"Well, remember … we are Frankie's A-team," Ruby pointed out. "We're probably already getting the best part of his business."

"But the key is, we don't know who his top clients were before we started working for him. There are probably all kinds of Daddy Warbucks' we can shake down," countered Satin.

"Fine," said Goldie. "Maybe I will be able to get a good attorney. Maybe I will be able to get a fair trial. But what if I lose?"

Satin smiled again. "It just so happens that last week, at the fundraiser, my 'date' for the night happened to be someone in power. And he wants to hook up with me again."

"Wow. Are you going to see him again?" asked Ruby.

Satin looked at her. "No. He was riddled with guilt — happily married, with a daughter. Claimed it was the first time outside his marriage. In fact, when I left here last week, I met him at Barnes & Noble to collect my fee. I have his fingerprints all over the cash as well as two books. Nice insurance to have in case Goldie does get caught — we may have to twist his arm. But one thing I do know is that he will do whatever I ask. He would be terrified if he thought his one-night stand with me was going to go public."

Goldie was beginning to feel a lot better. "Brilliant move, Satin. And we don't know who we'll turn up once we get Frankie's files, do we? There could be all kinds of judges, politicians, attorneys, and movie stars."

Ruby was curious. "What was the name of your powerful man, Satin? I saw you drinking with him at the bar, but I certainly didn't recognize him, since, like Goldie, I only saw him from the back."

Satin winked at her. "That will be my little secret, Ruby. Important thing is, Goldie, you're finally understanding the big picture when it comes to our new partnership. Just remember one very important thing, ladies- We're the ones holding all the cards."

CHAPTER 12

❝ **N**ow, both of you be good little girls while you're with your Auntie Margaret and Uncle Dave, OK?" Ruby said to Gabby and Maria as she pulled into the driveway at her sister's home.

"Yes, Mommy," both girls replied.

"And be sure to help your Auntie Margaret as much as you can tomorrow. As you know, it's the Fourth of July, and Auntie Margaret and Uncle Dave always have lots of company."

"We'll miss you, Mommy," said Gabby, wiping a tear from her eye.

Maria started to cry too.

"Nonsense, girls. You'll have lots of fun tomorrow watching the fireworks. You won't even notice I'm not there."

Dave and Margaret came out to greet them. Margaret noticed Ruby's wig. *What on earth possessed her to wear such a thing?* she thought, but decided to say nothing. David was not surprised by anything as it related to his sister-in-law. He stretched out his arms.

"And how are my favorite nieces? Come and give your Uncle David a big hug." Both girls ran to him and giggled as he kissed them on their cheeks.

"He's just a big old teddy bear," chuckled Ruby as she embraced her sister and eyed her slightly chubby and balding brother-in-law. "I am so pleased you've found real happiness, Margaret. You did well to marry Dave. He's such a gem."

Margaret detected a little wistfulness in her sister's voice. "Come on. Where are the girls' overnight bags?"

Ruby unlocked the trunk and removed their small suitcases. She reached in the back seat to retrieve the stuffed animals: Gabby's pink rabbit and Maria's little panda bear.

Margaret and Ruby headed for the house. Dave was already seated on the couch — one girl on each side of him — reading "Peter Pan."

Ruby dropped the cases at the doorway. "Do you have a goodbye kiss for Mommy?" Both girls quickly ran to their mother.

"I love you both," she said, wrapping her arms around them and squeezing them tightly. "Remember to be good now." The girls nodded.

She looked at her brother-in-law and blew him a kiss. "Thanks for everything, Dave. You're amazing."

He smiled back. "Come on, girls. Don't you want to know what is going on in Never, Never Land?" The girls ran back to him and snuggled up.

Margaret and Ruby walked back to the car. "I can tell you're worried — you have that look on your face," Ruby said to her sister.

"This is just so unlike you — to be spending a night and all of tomorrow away from your girls, especially on a holiday. You've never done it before."

"I'm fine, Margaret. Really, I am. There's nothing to worry about. I'll be by Monday morning to pick up the girls. I promise I won't be late. Thanks for everything."

Margaret hugged her sister. "Just take care of yourself, alright?"

Ruby climbed into her car and waved goodbye to Margaret before backing out onto the main street. She called Satin to let her know she was on her way.

"Just remember to drive past the house, make the first right, and almost immediately, take the first right into the alley. The Moyle's garage gate will be open. It's the third gate on the right. I'll be there."

"Wow, since you're the fourth house, I would have never figured out it's the third garage," said Ruby, poking fun at her friend.

"Sarcasm doesn't become you," replied Satin. "I'll see you there." She hung up, located the automatic garage opener, and headed quickly out the gate at the rear of her garden to open the garage for her friend. She stepped inside and, within a couple of minutes, heard Ruby's car turn into the garage from the alley.

"Perfect timing," said Satin. "None of the lights at the Kravitzes house are on, which means Gladys and Abner are out somewhere. Come on, let's get inside my house." She shut the garage, pushed Ruby down the little path, and followed her after she closed the gate.

"The Kravitzes?" asked Ruby. "Who the hell are the Kravitzes?"

"That's what I call my neighbors on the other side. Their real names are Sheila and Alan Godfrey. Remember Gladys and Abner Kravitz, the nosy neighbors in that old television series, *Bewitched*?

Ruby nodded.

"Sheila's the perfect Gladys Kravitz," Satin continued. "The only difference is, my neighbor's husband is equally as bad as she is. He's not the shy, withering, husband like Abner. No, both my neighbors suffer from Gladys Kravitz Syndrome. Want a drink before I run you back?"

Ruby chuckled at her friend's analysis of her neighbor. "Too funny. As for the drink, thanks all the same, but I'd just as soon get home. You can keep this here though. Figured I'll need to wear it tomorrow when Goldie and I go for our spin."

She removed her hairpiece and handed it to Satin, who placed it on the counter, grabbed the keys to her car from the key rack, and headed out. "By the way, where's the top you were supposed to bring for Goldie?"

"I'll bring it tomorrow. The girls would have noticed and started asking questions. It was easier not to deal with all that."

"You're not having second thoughts about this, are you?"

"No," replied Ruby, as she slammed the car door shut, much to Satin's annoyance. "In fact, if Goldie chickens out, I'll step in if need be. I've been counting down the days until the Fourth of July — and it's not just to celebrate our independence from the Brits. It's to celebrate our independence from Frankie. Every time I've spoken with him over the last couple of weeks, he's asked me about the girls." She started to mimic his sneering style. "How are your little beauties? Now be careful nothing happens to them, won't you? I wouldn't want *anything* to happen to them."

Satin shuddered. "What a scumbag. But I don't think you have to worry about Goldie backing out. I spoke to her this week. Frankie gave her another black eye. Poor kid will not be able to work for yet another week. She's fit to be tied and has so much anger and hatred toward him now — I just have a feeling that once she shoots from her gun, she won't stop until it's empty."

"Poor Goldie. I do feel for her." Ruby shook her head. "I still can't believe she has a gun though. I wonder where she got it. Hey, can't they trace bullets to a gun these days? And didn't she have to register the gun when she bought it? Or get a permit or something? I'm just not up on that stuff."

"Oh, I forgot. You don't know the story of Goldie's Colt 45. It belonged to a roommate of hers back in New York. When the roommate got killed, Goldie just took the gun. I guess she did it for self-preservation."

"I never knew that about Goldie. A roommate of hers got murdered? Jeez, she has had a tough life, hasn't she?"

They were quiet for a moment - the only sounds were the purr of the engine and the cars whizzing by outside.

"By this time tomorrow, it should all be over," said Ruby.

"Yup." Satin waved her hands through her hair. "And tomorrow we start to celebrate a new life and a new business venture together. Who would have thought?"

Ruby was pensive. "I hope the new business - with Goldie and all - doesn't change the dynamics of our friendship, Satin. We've been the best of friends for so long. We've been through a lot together."

Satin exited off the freeway toward Ruby's house. "It won't," she assured her. "We'll be able to run things better. We'll have a better life. We'll give all the girls a better break, and we'll make sure they're protected. There will be zero tolerance for the type of clients Goldie's been subjected to."

"Goldie will need to get off the drugs though."

"If she is serious in partnering with us, she must know in her heart of hearts that she's got to get clean, even if it means signing up with Narcanon."

"Agreed," said Ruby, as the car pulled up in front of her home. She leaned across to give her friend a hug. "I'm so glad our paths in life crossed, Satin."

"Me too. Until tomorrow. Don't forget the change of tops for Goldie."

"I won't. *Ciao*, my friend."

Satin sped off as Ruby unlocked her door. It was all so quiet. She went upstairs and looked inside the girls' bedroom. The house seemed hollow and empty. *Wow, this really feels weird not seeing my babies in their room.* She headed for her bedroom and sat on the side of the bed. As she removed her shoes, she decided to call Margaret.

"What's wrong? What's the matter?" Margaret asked. Her voice was shaky and implied a sense of urgency.

"Nothing, Sis. Relax. I just wanted to see how the girls were."

"Oh, thank God!" She sighed with relief. "They're fine. They fell asleep while Dave was reading to them, bless their little hearts. He carried them to their room and tucked them into bed. They didn't even stir."

Ruby smiled. "Thanks, Sis. Thanks again for always being there for me. And have a good day tomorrow. I know your party will be a huge success."

"Enjoy your Independence Day, too, Dear."

I will, thought Ruby. *I will.* "Goodnight, Margaret. I'll call you tomorrow." She hung up, finished undressing, washed her face, and climbed into bed.

Satin was almost at home when her phone rang.

It was Goldie. "We're still on tomorrow, right?", she asked in a surprisingly calm tone.

"Rain or shine!" Satin said. "I have everything ready for the barbecue. You just need to bring Ruby."

"And the champagne."

Satin understood the code Goldie was using. "If you wish," she said.

They said goodnight to each other and hung up. As Satin pulled into her garage, the lights were still out at the Godfrey's home. *Might just as well get the license plate taken care of and out of the way. One less thing to deal with tomorrow. Certainly, with Gladys and Abner gone, the timing is perfect.* Grabbing a screwdriver and the temporary license plate, she followed the path to the end of her garden and entered the Moyle's garage completely unnoticed. It was a matter of moments for her to change the plates. She returned home, poured herself a glass of wine, and headed for her bedroom. *I could really use a cosmopolitan. I just wish I wasn't too tired and lazy to make it.* Satin looked in the mirror, winked at herself, and raised her glass. "Cheers, kiddo. Here's to your new future."

She took a long sip from the glass, placed it on the bedside table, and climbed into bed. *I just hope we've thought of everything. Guess we have to pray all goes according to plan.*

CHAPTER 13

G oldie pulled up in front of Ruby's house and honked the horn.

"I'm coming, I'm coming," mumbled Ruby from inside her townhouse. She grabbed her bag, put on her sunglasses, removed the cake from the refrigerator, and locked the front door on her way out.

Goldie leaned across and opened the passenger car door. "Wow! Look at you, all Americana," she said, noting Ruby's white boots, blue denims, and red top.

"You're looking pretty patriotic yourself," Ruby replied. "Love your 'God Bless America' T-shirt."

Goldie put the car into gear and sped off.

With cat-like reflexes, Ruby immediately put her hand on her head. "Can you close the sunroof? I don't want my hair to get blown all over the place."

Goldie reached for the button above her. Ruby was relieved when the roof finally closed after what seemed like an eternity. "Thanks. Did you remember to pack the goodie?"

"Of course I did. What's in that box on your lap?"

"A Fourth of July cake. What kind of celebration is it without a cake?"

"Oh, my God. First the damn roses at the grave, and now a cake for every occasion. Who do you think you are? Ms. Manners? Martha Stewart?"

"No need to get snippy, Goldie. I'm just trying to make it a normal Independence Day celebration."

"I'm sorry, Honey." Goldie patted her friend on the knee. "I guess I'm just a little jumpy today. I bought some bubbly for the occasion."

Ruby studied her friend's face for the first time since getting into the car. *Actually, she's looking surprisingly serene — well, as serene as Goldie can look, I suppose.* "How are you feeling?" she asked in a quiet tone.

Goldie took a deep breath. "To be honest, I feel fine. Just knowing that creep will never, ever touch me again makes me feel at peace. You know what I mean? And I'm going to make damn sure he doesn't hurt anyone else either."

Ruby immediately thought about her two girls. "Yeah, I know what you mean," she said, her tone still soft. Not wanting to think about it anymore, she changed the subject. She looked at the mountains in the distance and the low-hanging clouds. "It's a beautiful day, isn't it? I can't help but think of all the picnics and festivities that will be happening across the valley, let alone the country."

"Yup," replied Goldie. "It feels good just to be alive."

In typical girl fashion, they talked … and talked … and talked until they arrived at their destination.

Satin heard the car arrive outside the house. She had been busy styling Goldie's wig. *I'm sure she's not going to like it. But what the hell? It's the best I can do. If Goldie doesn't like it, she can style it herself.* Satin went outside to greet her guests at the front gate, eyeing the neighbors' window on the way. *God is good,* she thought, as the Pearces peeked through their lace curtains. *Couldn't have asked for better timing.*

She hugged Goldie and Ruby, relieving them of the cake box and champagne. "Stay here at the gate," she whispered. "The Kravitzes are watching from their window."

"So pleased you could make it!" Satin said, switching to her outside voice. "Wait here. I'll just put these inside and

I'll be back. I'd love to show you my garden." She disappeared into the house.

"Who the hell are the Kravitzes?" muttered Goldie.

"They're Satin's neighbors. Their real names are Sheila and Alan Godfrey, I think. Satin calls them the Kravitzes. They're our alibi."

Before Goldie had a chance to fully grasp the neighbors' dual identities, Satin emerged from the house.

"Your garden looks beautiful," Ruby exclaimed, as if on cue. "We'd love you to show us around."

The three of them slowly started around the perimeter of the yard, Satin halting at various locations to highlight some of the assorted blooms. She took extra care to stop at the closest point to the Pearces' window, discussing at length the difficulty of growing pansies with such restrictive water rationing. Ruby and Goldie were instructed to look up so the Pearces could get a good look at their faces. *Mission accomplished,* Satin thought. She smiled and waved at her neighbors, who let go of the drapes and walked away.

The three musketeers went inside.

"Perfect, perfect, perfect!" Satin said, clapping her hands enthusiastically. "Who wants a celebratory drink?" She grabbed three glasses, reached into the refrigerator, pulled out a bottle of champagne, and popped the cork. "We'll save your champagne for later, Goldie." She filled the glasses and handed them to her friends. "To the land of the free," toasted Satin.

"And the home of the brave" said Ruby, clinking her glass.

"And to Frankie — may he never rest in peace," said Goldie, raising her glass to the others.

"Wow! Now that's cold," said Ruby, trying to stifle a chuckle.

"As he will be in a short while," said Goldie flatly.

"Let's go sit outside on the front porch," said Satin. "The Pearces will be out on their porch soon. The more they see us, the better."

Goldie suddenly noticed the wig on the couch. "Please tell me that's not what I'm supposed to be wearing today, Satin." She gingerly picked up the wig with two fingers and eyed it with disdain. "I wouldn't be caught dead in this thing."

Satin patted her on the back with her free hand. "Just point the gun in the right direction, and you won't be. We don't want you to be caught dead at all. We want you to be alive, get the job done, get back here, and enjoy the barbecue. But since this is the land of the free ... feel free to style the wig, if you wish. I put an old pair of gloves there for you to wear, too, so you don't get your fingerprints on anything."

"If I lived till doomsday, I couldn't manage to make this thing look like a hairstyle," Goldie said with a disgusted look on her face, ignoring the comment about the gloves.

"When it's time for you to get ready, I'll help," offered Ruby. "But right now, I think Satin's right; we need to go sit outside for a while to be seen. By the way, Satin, where's my wig? Never mind, I see it on the table over there."

As Satin had suspected, the Kravitzes were on their porch. Their chairs were strategically positioned at an angle to see Satin's house, without appearing too obvious. But Satin wasn't fooled. She knew exactly what they were doing.

The three women chatted nonchalantly for a short while, Satin popping back and forth to replenish champagne and refill the chips and dip. Finally, it was time to put their plan into action. "Well, I think it's time to get the barbecue going," Satin announced loudly.

"What can we do to help?" asked Ruby, picking up the chip and dip bowls.

"I need one of you to chop the ingredients for the fruit salad and the potato salad. And whoever's left can start the grill while I set the table."

Satin could almost sense the Kravitzes straining their ears, but she made sure she was speaking loud enough for them to hear. The three of them disappeared indoors.

"When the hell are we going to get all that done?" asked Goldie. She was beginning to panic.

"Calm down," said Satin. "It's already done; everything's in the fridge. Those were just excuses to come inside. I'm going out the back garden to light the grill. You start getting changed, Goldie. You can help her, Ruby."

She switched on the TV to the channel showing the celebration from Washington, D.C., and turned up the volume loud enough so their voices couldn't be heard next door.

Ruby was already reshaping the wig. "I'm seeing if I can do anything with this."

"Where's my top?" asked Goldie.

"Oh, my God! I forgot! It's underneath the cardboard base of the cake in the fridge. I hid it there, so no one would see it when we arrived."

"You're kidding me, right?" Goldie stared at her, an incredulous look on her face. "As if the lousy wig isn't bad enough, now I'm going to have to wear a freezing-cold blouse?"

"Oh, stop," interjected Satin, removing the cake box from the fridge. "Oh, my! What a beautiful cake. Thank you, Ruby. It's so Fourth of July." She lifted the cake and retrieved the blouse from underneath.

Goldie snatched the ice-cold blouse from Satin's hands and held it up. "Are you both insane? Look at this! A dreary, tri-colored blouse. I thought it was supposed to be plain. It looks as if the pattern was taken from a cardboard container of Neapolitan ice cream."

Ruby was offended. "Well, at least it's silk."

"It's silk? No, it's not. It's crap. I'm not wearing it," retorted Goldie.

"I must admit, it's not exactly … inconspicuous," added Satin. "Let me see what I can find upstairs. Why don't the two of you go outside and get the grill started?"

"I'll get the grill started," offered Ruby, since she really didn't want to be alone with Goldie at that point. "Why don't you see what you can do with the wig, Goldie?"

Satin soon returned with a plain, pale blue blouse. It was not one she really wanted to part with, but time was of the essence. Goldie quickly slipped into it, fitted the wig, put on the gloves, and donned her sunglasses. She stepped into the nearby bathroom to check herself out in the mirror. "I guess I look OK," she said in a begrudging manner.

"Point is, nobody would recognize you. That's the key," Satin reminded her.

Ruby returned from the back garden. "I'm sorry if I let the team down, but Satin's right, Goldie. No one would recognize you."

"OK, my fellow business partners," Satin said and smiled. "I'm now going out front to set the table. If the Kravitzes are there, I'll invite them to join us for the barbecue. If you hear a line of conversation in that fashion, it will be your cue to leave. I just want to make sure that neither of them has gone upstairs for anything. It's simply an extra precaution, since that's the only place they can see you beyond the high wall."

Goldie picked up her purse as Ruby donned and adjusted her own wig.

"Wait a minute! You can't take that purse. The Kravitzes would have seen that when you arrived. Let me get you a shoulder bag. You'll need a larger one, anyway, for Frankie's files." Satin disappeared but quickly returned with a sturdy, deep, fake leather bag. Goldie emptied the contents of her purse into the bag.

They all hugged each other tightly, Ruby and Satin wishing Goldie luck.

Satin picked up the checkered tablecloth, along with the napkins and the silverware, and took them outside. The sun was beginning to set. *Gladys and Abner are so true to form,* she thought. *I could have staked my own life that they'd be sitting outside to see what's happening.* "My friends and I are having a little barbecue tonight," she yelled across to them "Nothing fancy, just some hamburgers, hot dogs, potato salad, fruit salad, and — of course — cake. You know, typical Fourth of July stuff. There's plenty here. You're welcome to join us."

Ruby and Goldie were on their way.

"That's very sweet of you, my dear," Sheila said. "But we wouldn't dream of intruding, would we, Alan?"

"Of course not," Alan chimed in. "That would be an imposition. But a happy Independence Day to you, anyway."

Satin smiled. "Well, if you change your mind, we'll probably be eating in about an hour's time. Just come on over." She took her time setting the table.

"There's something weird going on there, Al," Sheila said quietly.

"Perhaps you shouldn't have turned down the invite so quickly," he replied.

"We can always change our minds. Let's see what happens."

Back inside her house, Satin opened the refrigerator, removed the plate of hamburger patties and hot dogs, and took them outside by the grill. As she busied herself by arranging condiments into a set of matching bowls, she heard Tchaikovsky's 1812 overture playing on the TV. *Right now, Goldie should be pulling the trigger. Oh Goldie, I pray you're not caught.* For just a moment, her nerves got the better of her. But she knew that worrying wasn't going to do her any good now. So, she did the next best thing - filled her champagne glass and disappeared into the back garden to prepare for the celebration.

Across the city, Ruby dropped Goldie off at Frankie's office building. Just like they planned, she drove around the block a few times before parking across the street. A few early fireworks were shooting off at various points of the skyline. Ruby hoped this would provide her with a nice distraction, but she, too, was preoccupied worrying about Goldie.

Goldie entered the building and took the stairs to the second floor. Outside of Frankie's office, she could hear the TV playing loudly. As Satin had told her, he was listening to the program from the nation's capital. Sound was clearly emanating from a second TV, as she also heard the excited voice of a baseball announcer yelling "It's going, it's going, and it's gone! Grand slam! Home run ..." She did not hear the rest, as the roar of the crowd drowned out the name of the player. Not that she cared. She opened the door and walked in.

Frankie was seated at his desk, facing her, cellphone to his ear, engaged in conversation. He looked up and threw his free hand in the air. "Well, well, well," he said partly to his visitor and partly into the mouthpiece. "You'll never guess who we have here. In fact, just exactly who *do* we have here?"

"Who is it, Frankie?" came a voice from the mouthpiece, "Who is it?"

CHAPTER 14

G oldie didn't hear a word Frankie said. She headed straight toward him, reached into the bag, grabbed the Colt 45, pointed it at him, and fired two shots directly at his chest. Frankie slumped forward, dropping the phone onto his desk. Blood oozed from his mouth.

Goldie stopped for a moment. The TV was still playing the finale of Tchaikovsky's 1812 Overture, with the bells ringing and the fireworks thundering in the background. As she approached the desk, she heard the same concerned female voice on the cellphone as she had when she first walked in.

"Frankie, are you there? Frankie, can you hear me? Hello? Hello?"

For the love of God, shut up woman! Goldie grabbed the phone from the desk, planning to terminate the call, but immediately thought better of it. *I think I'll leave her squawking. The dingbat must have heard the shots. But while she's screaming in the phone, at least she's not calling 911.* She put the phone back on the desk, grabbed Frankie's laptop, and stuffed it in the oversize bag. *Good thinking on the bigger bag, Satin.* She opened all of the drawers in his desk, removed what appeared to be journals and address books, and threw them in with the laptop. *I'll check these out later.*

"Frankie, please tell me you're all right." The persistent voice on the phone was more plaintive than ever.

Goldie picked up the phone, disconnected the call, and dropped the cell in her bag. *Just drop dead, Bitch.* She picked up the keys from the desk and strode toward the filing cabinet, noticing a closed, black leather suitcase on the nearby couch as she went. *Great, I might just need that.*

The landline started ringing. Goldie figured it was the same woman from the cellphone. *Damn, that voice was familiar, but I can't place it right now. I can't even think about it right now.* She fumbled with the keys, and after three attempts, the cabinet opened. She scanned through the folders on the top layer. *Not a damn thing here.* Her hand pulled open the middle drawer. *Thank God for these gloves. Gee, Satin really did think of everything.* As her fingers flicked through all the folders, the names of celebrities, politicians, and other well-known people blew her mind. *Bingo! I think I've hit the jackpot.* She quickly grabbed the suitcase from the couch, unzipped it, and emptied the clothes on the floor. *Huh, looks like Frankie was going somewhere. Well, I guess we've just changed his destination. Enjoy your trip, Frankie.*

The phone on the desk stopped ringing. *Yikes, I better get out of here. If it's the same person who was on the phone, she's probably about to call the police.*

She threw the folders into the case and quickly opened the bottom drawer. There was yet another stack of folders, this section displaying the names of some of her colleagues. She snatched up the pile and tossed them into the suitcase with the rest of them. She zipped the suitcase, shut the drawers, threw the keys back on Frankie's desk, and ran to the front door. *Wait a minute,* she thought. *There's no point in leaving the keys and making it easy for the police to investigate.* She went back for the keys, flashed the lights on and off twice, and made her way along the corridor. The two TVs were still blaring, but the sound faded as she made her exit. Given the extra luggage, Goldie decided to take the elevator. She pressed the button multiple times. A police siren could be heard in the distance. *Come on, come on, come on,* she muttered to the inanimate elevator, as if that would speed it up. When the elevator finally arrived, she feared Ruby would be gone.

When Ruby saw the flashing lights, she put her car into reverse, pulled out of the parking lot, and drove across the road. Goldie was not at the rendezvous yet, so she parked outside the building and left the engine running. A loud bang on her window startled her. When she turned to look, her eyes met those of a disheveled man. He held a dilapidated cardboard sign against his face. *homeless veteran. please help. will work for food. God bless you.*

Ruby glared at him, with his unkempt hair, dingy beard, and grubby-looking mustache. "You nearly scared me half to death!" she stammered as she rummaged through her purse. She grabbed a bill and, without even checking the denomination, rolled down the window and handed it to him. "Now go away, and leave me alone."

"God bless you, Ma'am." He scratched his head before stuffing the bill into his tattered shirt pocket.

As he ambled in front of the car to the curb, Ruby noticed Goldie hurrying toward the car. *What in the world is she doing with a suitcase?* She reached back to open the rear door just as Goldie heaved the bags inside.

As soon as Goldie climbed into the front seat, they sped off. The siren suddenly sounded much louder. Goldie saw the police car pull up in front of the building from her side mirror. It did not go unnoticed by Ruby, who saw the same thing in the rearview mirror.

"Should we be worried?" she asked. "Did something happen?"

"Nah. All went according to plan. Except … when I arrived … Frankie was talking on his cellphone. No doubt the person he was talking to heard the shots. I'm sure whoever was on the other end of that call is the one who alerted the police."

"Shots?"

"I shot him twice."

"Well, we were already on our way when the police car pulled up, so I don't think they would suspect us. We're just people traveling somewhere for the Fourth. Did everything else go all right?"

"Yes. But let's talk about it when we get back to Satin's. That way, I won't need to go through everything twice. Anyway, who was that pistol of a guy you were chatting up when I came out of the building? Scoring a date for tomorrow night?"

"Don't be funny, Goldie. This is not the time for humor. What the hell's in the suitcase? Frankie?"

"I was just trying to lighten things up, and you come up with a crack like that?"

"Never mind. How did it go?"

"Well, the deed is done. All went according to plan. Frankie's gone. History. I do hope Satin's got the food under way. I'm starving."

Ruby marveled at Goldie's way of compartmentalizing situations. She had just killed a man, and here she was thinking about her stomach. *Must be the result of having had such a hard life,* she reasoned. "Don't worry. I'm sure the barbecue will all be ready as soon as we walk through the door," she said to her friend.

As she turned onto the freeway, she put her foot on the accelerator. *I can't wait to get to Satin's to hear the details.*

Goldie lit a cigarette. For the first time, her hand started to shake a little. She rummaged in the bag for Frankie's cellphone, and busied herself removing the SIM card.

CHAPTER 15

S atin looked at her watch. *If everything went according to plan, they should be back any moment now.* She flipped the hamburgers one last time before removing and placing them on a platter with the hot dogs. As she carried everything into the kitchen, her cellphone rang. She recognized the number. "Well, well, well. Judge Richard … this is quite a surprise."

"I hope it's a pleasant one," he said, in a tone that gave her goosebumps. "I just finished watching the celebration in Washington, D.C., on TV. Something about the music and the fireworks captivates me."

"Me too. I watch it every year." She paused to see what he would say next.

"Well," he said sheepishly, "I just wanted to give you a call and wish you a happy Fourth."

"That's sweet. Aren't you spending the day with your wife and Deidre?"

"I'm impressed you remember my daughter's name."

"All part of my charm," she teased. "Look, I can't stay and chat. I have company. We're having a barbecue."

"I guess I just wanted you to know that as I watched the fireworks on TV, I remembered the fireworks we made together, and … Well, I hope we can do it again sometime."

"Perhaps." She heard Ruby's car driving up the back alley. "I'm sorry, but I have to go. Can we finish this conversation later?"

"Enjoy the fireworks."

"You too."

They hung up.

While Ruby and Goldie were gone, Satin went back and forth from the house to her porch, carrying rolls, condiments, salads — everything she could, one by one — to make sure she knew where the neighbors were at all times. She quickly peered outside to see if they were still sitting on the porch, then dashed to the kitchen door. She was confused to hear the sound of three doors closing after the roar of the engine died down. *What in the world is in that suitcase Goldie's carrying?* Before saying anything, Satin gave Goldie an impenetrable hug.

Ruby hurried to the bathroom and quickly removed her wig. "Goldie did good," she said, fluffing her hair, and returning to the kitchen. She casually carried the plate of burgers and hot dogs to the porch, where she could be seen. "Everything look's delicious!" she hollered.

"C'mon, Goldie," said Satin. "Let's get you back into your clothes, and then you can tell us everything that happened."

I'd rather die than wear these clothes for a second longer, Goldie thought, as she hastily wrangled her way out of the gloves and top.

Satin grabbed the garments and scurried to the back garden to dispose of the evidence in the smoldering barbecue. When she returned, she noticed Goldie had already dispensed with the wig and combed her hair back into place.

"Here, take these out onto the patio," Satin instructed, handing her two clean champagne flutes. She took Goldie's bottle of champagne from the refrigerator and another glass from the counter. The two joined Ruby on the front porch.

"Wow, this all looks fabulous!" Goldie said, genuinely. "I'm starving!"

Satin popped the champagne cork, filled the glasses, and the three of them sat down to hear Goldie's story and celebrate their newfound freedom.

Goldie spoke softly, with her back to neighbor's house, making it difficult for the Kravitzes to hear her. The TV inside was still broadcasting Sousa marches and other patriotic music. Fortunately, the volume was loud enough to dominate their conversation. Still, with her back to the neighbor's house, Goldie spoke ever so softly, very carefully describing every single detail. Ruby and Satin were spellbound as they listened to the story of Frankie's last breath.

"Seems to me the only thing we need to worry about is the homeless bum," Satin said confidently, after Goldie finished her story.

Ruby wiped her mouth with a napkin. "Don't think we need to worry about him. Doubt if he knows what day of the week it is. I'm more concerned as to who was calling Frankie on the Fourth of July. I mean, who in the hell would spend any holiday talking to Frankie?"

Goldie was enjoying her hamburger. "We can find out who that was by looking at the log on Frankie's cell. Remember, I have it in the bag Satin gave me. We can do that after dinner. We'll have to replace the SIM card."

Ruby had other thoughts on her mind. "Aren't either of you worried about the police?"

"We don't even know for sure if they were there for Frankie. I'm more anxious to see who's in the files you've got in that suitcase and what information Frankie has in his laptop," mused Satin.

The three of them continued to discuss Frankie's demise and the future of their new business venture until it was time for dessert.

"Cake time," said Satin, loudly enough for her neighbors to hear.

The three of them set about putting away the plates and condiments in the kitchen before returning to the porch.

Satin sliced the patriotically designed gateau and handed the first two plates to Goldie. "Here," she said loudly. "Why don't you take these to Alan and Sheila? We're going to be in trouble if we eat all this ourselves!"

Goldie sensed the cue and took the plates to the fence. She smiled at the nosy neighbors. *I can see why Satin dislikes these suburban creeps.* "Satin thought you might like a piece of this delicious Fourth of July cake."

Sheila nudged her husband. Alan came to the fence and took the paper plates. "Why, thank you. Mighty kind of you." He looked over at Satin and repeated his thanks.

Goldie could tell he was being fake — with his phony grin and all. *What a jerk.* "You're so welcome," she said, giving him one last smile before she turned to join her friends again.

As soon as they had finished the cake and champagne, they cleared the table and went inside. Goldie started to get fidgety.

Satin was throwing the paper plates into the trash bin. "Are you OK, Honey?"

"I just need my fix."

Knowing Satin had none of the white powder she craved, Goldie rummaged in her purse for a cigarette.

Satin stopped what she was doing and led Goldie to the couch in the living room. As soon as they sat down, Goldie suddenly burst into tears. The realization of what she had done had suddenly dawned on her.

"My God. How I loathed and hated Frankie. But I never thought I could kill anyone. I guess … I can. I'm a cold-blooded murderer!" Her hands trembled as she lit a cigarette.

Satin put her arms around Goldie to comfort her. "Ruby, please get the box of tissues from the bathroom."

Ruby left, returned with the tissues in hand, and sat the other side of her weeping friend. "Goldie, you just did what you had to do. It had to be done. We're all in this together."

"But I was the one who pulled the trigger. Not once, but twice. And you know what the frightening part is? I could have just as easily emptied the gun." Goldie rested her cigarette in the ashtray and grabbed some tissues from the box.

Ruby and Satin were quiet as they contemplated the consequences of their actions. Aside from Goldie's sniffing, the only sound that could be heard was that of the soprano singing "America the Beautiful" emanating from the television.

Finally, Satin broke the silence. "Why don't you spend the night here?"

Goldie collected herself and shook her head. *Maybe if I hunt hard enough, I might find something stronger than a cigarette at home.* "No, I'll be fine. But thank you! Actually, I think I should get home now. It's been a long day."

"Are you sure? You can stay with me too," Ruby offered. "The girls aren't there."

Goldie smiled weakly. "I'll be fine. Really I will. Let's help Satin clean up."

"No, I've got everything. You go ahead. Let's make sure Gladys and Abner Kravitz get to see you one more time."

Ruby and Goldie laughed.

"Thanks, Satin. I needed that chuckle," Goldie said as she extinguished her forgotten cigarette, which had turned into ash. "Come on, Ruby. Let's get our things and head home." Both ladies picked up their purses.

"Ruby, do you want to take the rest of the cake for the girls?" Satin asked.

"No thanks, Honey, you keep it."

The three of them headed out toward the car, laughing, chatting, and exchanging thanks as they went. Satin was pleased to notice the neighbors still sitting on their porch. They hugged and kissed each other goodbye as Ruby and Goldie got into the car.

"Give my love to the girls," Satin yelled as the car sped off. She turned and headed back inside the house, waving to her neighbors. "Good-night," she yelled.

"The cake was lovely. Thank you," said Sheila.

Satin feigned a smile. "Glad you liked it."

Once inside, she noticed that the Independence Day ceremonies on the TV had concluded, so she switched the station to a local channel. She checked the barbecue grill outside to make sure the clothes had disintegrated into ashes and that there were no smoldering embers. Returning to the kitchen, she kept herself busy cleaning up and listening to the seemingly endless, inane commercials on the air. She rinsed the crystal champagne flutes in warm water. As she started to dry them, the news broke.

"Good evening everyone, and welcome to your local Action News. Today, a man was found dead in his Las Vegas office building. The police have determined it was a homicide. The identity of the man is being withheld pending notification to his immediate family. In other news this evening…"

Satin dropped one of the glasses on the floor. *Oh, my God. So, the police sirens Ruby and Goldie heard* **were** *going to Frankie's office.* She suddenly realized they forgot to check Frankie's phone log. She hurried to the living room, where they left the suitcase. *Amazing, Goldie thought to switch the phone off.* She reinstalled the SIM card, powered it on, waited impatiently for it to warm up, and quickly accessed the call log. Satin recognized the name immediately. It hit her like a lightning bolt. *Well, I'll be a son of a gun.* She immediately powered off the phone and removed the SIM card.

CHAPTER 16

S atin couldn't wait to divulge the details of Frankie's last conversation to Ruby and Goldie. But, as a safety precaution, she decided not to do it over the phone.

As planned, Satin picked Ruby up from her house the next morning to retrieve her car from the Moyle's garage.

"I guess you heard about Frankie," Satin said as soon as Ruby closed the door.

"How could I not? It's all over the news."

"How was Goldie on the drive home? I wanted to call her, but decided better not to."

"She seemed OK. For the most part, I think she was just hankering for some cocaine. We have to get her off that."

"Agreed. I'll try and stop by and see her later today. Not sure it's a good idea to communicate on phones right now. And speaking of phones, you'll never guess who was on the phone with Frankie yesterday for a whole 45 minutes when Goldie interrupted the call?" She paused for effect, glancing at Ruby for reaction. "None other than our little newbie, Pearl."

"Pearl? What the hell is she trying to do, put us all out of a job? Frankie's already handed her a couple of my regulars."

"Mine too. But Pearl is young, and now she's in way over her head. Once the police start interrogating her, she'll freak out. Remember — she's still young and naïve in the ways of the world."

"Are you going to call her?"

"No. I'll wait for her to call me. After she's been grilled by the police, she'll be on the phone wanting to know what to do. When I've finished with her, she'll be hightailing it back to that little town in Ohio or Indiana, or wherever it is she comes from."

"Does she have your phone number?"

"If she doesn't, she'll get it. She's resourceful, I'll give her that. She'll probably get it from my regular Bellagio client, who Frankie turned over to her. Nice thing is, we don't have to worry about servicing clients anymore. We just have to find someone to provide the service."

They both laughed, but Ruby turned serious again quickly.

"Goldie gave me the gun yesterday. When I pick up the girls, I'm going to drive up to Bryce Canyon in Utah for a couple of days."

"Isn't tonight your night with Daddy Warbucks — the banker?"

"He went away for the long weekend. Wanted me to go with him."

"Got it. Why are you going to Bryce Canyon?"

"I need a couple of days away, and I want to spend some time with the girls. Bryce Canyon seems to be away from it all. While we're there, we can drive to Panguitch Lake, hire a boat, and I can drop the gun over the side. I know the girls would rather go to Disneyland, but I'll make it up to them another time. They'll enjoy the boat ride."

"Good thinking. While you're there, you can drop Frankie's cell over the side, too. I took all the names, numbers, and email addresses from his contact list and wrote them all down. I was up half the night. Some of his contacts are really eye-popping, by the way. I know the police will ransack his house. They'll probably uncover the same information from some computer he has lying around. But we don't want to make it any easier for them."

"Yes, I'm fully expecting the police to start harassing us too. They'll probably get search warrants and turn our places upside down."

"I think we can outsmart them."

Satin turned the car onto the street where she lived. "Duck down, Ruby. The Kravitzes are pulling out of their driveway. We can't let them see you."

Ruby quickly leaned forward, placing her head between her knees. Satin smiled and waved to her neighbors as their cars passed each other. As they turned the corner into the back alley, Satin opened the Moyle's garage door with the remote. Ruby sat up and ran her fingers through her hair to straighten it. Satin fumbled through her purse and pulled out Frankie's cellphone. "Here. Take this and the SIM card."

Ruby grabbed both items, pushed them down to the bottom of her purse, and climbed out of the car. Satin drove around the block, through the back alley again, and closed the garage door as she saw Ruby's car turn the corner and disappear from view.

Ruby drove back to her house and picked up an overnight suitcase and a change of clothing for the girls before leaving to go to her sister's house. *I wonder if Margaret has heard the news. Sure am glad I never told her I worked for an escort agency. She'd really be fretting.* As soon as she pulled up in front of the house, Maria and Gabby came running out to meet her, clutching their stuffed animals. "Mommy, Mommy, we missed you," they yelled, wrapping their arms around her, holding on for dear life.

"I missed you, too, my darlings. Were you on your best behavior with your Auntie Margaret and Uncle David?"

"They sure were," interjected Margaret. "Do you have time for some coffee?"

"Thanks, but I must run. Come on, in you go, and stay here while I get your suitcases." She opened the passenger doors for the girls before going into the house with her sister.

Margaret had a worried expression on her face. "You don't know that man who was killed last night, do you? It's been all over the news today."

Ruby gave her a hug. "You worry far too much. I wish I could stop, but I'm taking the girls to Bryce Canyon for a couple of days. Just to get away and spend some time with them."

"Oh, they'll love it there. Well, you just travel safely now, OK?"

"We will. Thank you for everything, and give my love to Dave." She hurried along the path and loaded the suitcases into the back of the car. "Wave goodbye to your Auntie Margaret and thank her."

"Bye, Auntie Margaret. Thank you," the girls yelled, almost in unison.

Ruby broke the news of the surprise trip to her girls.

"What's Bryce Canyon?" asked Gabby.

"I'd rather go to Disneyland," grumbled Maria.

"You'll both love Bryce Canyon. It's a beautiful park, not far from a very pretty lake, where we can rent a boat."

The girls remained subdued and crestfallen.

"We can even take a pony ride if you like," Ruby continued.

Maria and Gabby were unconvinced. Ruby turned the car onto the freeway signaling the direction of Mesquite. "I know you will have a great time when we get there. Now, why don't you tell me about your sleepover with Auntie Margaret and Uncle David?"

Both girls sprang to life, talking over each other about all the excitement of the previous day. In no time at all, they had forgotten about Disneyland.

*****

Damn, I need a fix. Goldie lit a cigarette and moved restlessly around her home. She was grateful when Satin showed up unexpectedly.

"Dear God, you look like a nervous wreck," Satin said when Goldie opened the door.

"I'm hoping to hear from Harvey. I need my fix. Harvey's good to me when it comes to that. Want some coffee?"

Satin grabbed her by the arms and pulled her onto the sofa.

"Hey! You're going to have to kick this addiction, Goldie! There's too much at stake. It's only a matter of time before the police start questioning us. We need you to get your act together. And not only that, you need to do it for yourself."

Goldie toyed with her hair. "I don't think I can stop now. I wouldn't know how. Let me get you some coffee." She jumped up from the seat and went into the kitchen.

Satin followed her. "You have to find a way, Goldie, for your own salvation. Why don't you go to Narcanon? Ruby and I will come with you, if you like. We can at least offer moral support."

Goldie perked up a little. "You promise you'll come with me? You and Ruby would do that?"

"Of course we would. You call and set up the appointment, and we'll be there for you. I promise."

Goldie was heartened, but suspicious. "OK. Maybe I'll call them after you leave."

"No. You need to promise that you'll make that commitment and take that giant first step."

"All right, all right. I promise I'll do it." Goldie was agitated and lit another cigarette. She was done talking about drugs. "I wonder what Ruby is going to do with the gun?"

"Didn't she tell you?"

"She may have told me last night. I was a bit foggy on the drive home."

"She's off to Panguitch Lake with the girls. She's going to drop it in the lake, along with Frankie's phone — and the SIM card from it. Last night, I chopped the wigs up, and on my way here today, I stopped at a couple of mini-malls and dropped some in each of the garbage cans outside the shops. I'll stop at a couple on the way home, too. By the way, do I have some names for you as to some of Frankie's clients? I'll share them with you and Ruby next time we're together. Do you think we should have a wig meeting?"

"Whatever. I can't focus right now."

"Don't worry. I'll set it up — Saturday afternoon at the cemetery. I'll call Ruby when she gets back to let her know. I'll fill you both in there."

Noticing Goldie's obvious disinterest, she switched subjects. "You know, at first, I thought we shouldn't communicate with each other by phone. But I think that may seem unnatural, you know, if our records are checked. So I think we should call each other like we normally would. What were you thinking when you heard it on the news last night?"

"Actually, I didn't. I came in and went straight to bed. I was so exhausted. I thought I was going to toss and turn all night, but I slept like a log. I heard it on the news this morning. Boy, they were all over the story. I had to switch the TV off. I think that's why I'm feeling a bit jumpy today."

Her phone rang. Seeing it was Harvey, she quickly answered it, holding her hand over the receiver. "Excuse me, Satin. It's Harvey." She disappeared from the kitchen and went into her bedroom.

Within seconds, Satin's phone rang. She looked at the phone and recognized Pearl's phone number. *What the hell does she want?* she wondered, and let it go into voicemail. As soon as the message appeared, she played it back. Satin smirked. *Have I got news for you, little Miss Pearl? I'll call you when I get home.*

There was a muffled sound emanating from the bedroom. Satin, figuring it might be a while, scribbled a quick note to Goldie and left. When Goldie finally finished her call with Harvey, she returned to the kitchen and picked up Satin's note.

Thanks for the coffee. Must run. Have much to do today. Will see you Saturday, and we'll chat before. Don't forget to call Narcanon. Ciao.

Goldie ripped up the note. She didn't care. She had a date with Harvey that night. She knew he would have more than cash for her. Her world suddenly seemed brighter.

CHAPTER 17

Satin detoured on her way home, stopping off at a couple of mini-malls, dispensing the remaining snippets of the wigs. She kicked off her shoes as she walked through her front door, put her purse on the counter, and headed straight to the refrigerator to make herself a lunchtime snack. *That leftover fruit salad looks good*, she thought, turning on the small TV in the kitchen and spooning herself a generous serving of the fruit.

My God, I can't believe this constant news over the death of Frankie. Anyone would think he was the patron saint of virtue or something, the way they're carrying on. She immediately switched the TV off and savored her snack. The phone rang. Satin left her lunch, reached inside her purse to retrieve her cell, and immediately recognized Pearl's number — again. Pushing the fruit salad to the side, she answered the phone this time.

"What is it, Pearl?"

"Thank God, I finally got through to you, Satin. Didn't you get the message I left earlier?"

"Yes." Satin reached inside her purse again and lit up a cigarette.

"Why the hell didn't you call me back? Have you heard the news about Frankie?"

Satin exhaled. "Yes, I heard the news about Frankie."

"What are we going to do? I had the police on the phone last night. They've been over here today, interrogating me. Can you believe it? Literally interrogating me."

Satin recognized the sound of panic when she heard it. "And what did you tell them?"

"I don't know. I can't remember. I was confused. There were two of them shooting questions at me left and right. Satin, what are we going to do?"

Satin was enjoying every minute of the phone call. "Well, if you can't handle the heat, you need to get out of the kitchen, Sweetie. Why don't you just head on back to Ohio or Indiana or wherever it is that you came from?"

"I'm from Arkansas. A little town called Magnolia."

"That's right. Now, why don't you just pack your bags and head on back to little old Magnolia — back to mommy and daddy?"

"Satin, why are you talking to me like this? I don't want to go back home. I want to stay here and work. I like my job, and I'm good at it."

"No, you're not good at what you do, Pearl. I saw you at that fundraiser for the homeless, making yourself the center of attention — all the men swarming around you like bees to honey. You're not discreet. You're not subtle. Now why don't you just run along home, like I suggested?"

Pearl was taken aback. "Satin, the reason I called you is to find out what we can all do together? Obviously, one of Frankie's girls killed him. We all need to protect each other. You're the only one of Frankie's girls I know who has access to all of our phone numbers. That's why I gave the police your number."

Satin was furious. "You did what? What the hell did you do that for?"

"I didn't know what else to do."

"Pearl, you listen to me, and you listen to me good. You're in way over your head. Now you just pack your bags and get the hell out of this town — and do it now. Do you hear me?"

She heard Pearl crying on the other end of the phone. *Sniveling twit*, she thought as she lowered the phone from her ear and hung up.

Satin tossed the rest of her snack down the garbage disposal. She had completely lost her appetite. As she headed into her living room, she saw a police car turning onto her street. She ran as fast as she could, zipped Frankie's suitcase containing all the files, and hid it securely in the Moyle's garage. *Better make sure everything is out of sight — and out of reach — from the police.* The doorbell rang as she made her way back through her garden. It rang a second time almost instantaneously. *My God, they're impatient.* She took a deep breath and answered the door.

"Good afternoon, Officer." Her manner was calm. "I've been expecting you."

CHAPTER 18

Goldie headed to where Ruby and Satin were already waiting, treading carefully around the gravesites, as if walking through a minefield.

"Good grief, Goldie, that's the mangiest arrangement of flowers I've ever seen." Satin watched her friend place the slightly wilted gerbera daisies and baby's breath by the headstone.

"Best I could manage, given the short notice Ruby gave me to pick up some flowers. I had to stop by the supermarket. That's pretty much all that was available. It's not like the person resting here is a good friend of ours, for Pete's sake."

Satin lit a cigarette. "Never mind. We have more important things to discuss. How did it go at Panguitch Lake, Ruby?"

Ruby removed her sunglasses, took a small cloth from her purse, and started cleaning them. "It was great. At our cabin in Bryce Canyon, there were some sizeable rocks outside. I used one of them to smash the SIM card from Frankie's phone. It was in a thousand pieces when I sprinkled it out the car window on the drive to Panguitch. The girls were having so much fun on the boat ride, they were completely unaware when I dropped the gun in the water. I waited until we were on the opposite side of the lake before I threw the phone in. But I did receive a visit from a Detective Bill Cooper yesterday. He kind of freaked me out.

How did he get my name? And equally important, how did he get my address?"

Goldie was somewhat relieved. "Yeah, he came to my house too. I wondered how he was on to me so quickly. I thought I'd been singled out." She was nervous again and started playing with the buttons on her blouse while reliving the detective's visit.

"Relax, girls," Satin said as she fanned her hands to calm her troubled friends. "You can thank Pearl, our little Miss Magnolia Queen, for that. She called me, fretting over the fact that the police were now badgering her. She gave the detective the names and phone numbers of all of Frankie's escorts. Well, those she knew, anyway … the dumb twit."

"Wait till I get my hands on her," Goldie interrupted. "Indiscreet trash that she is. She could blow the whole thing." For a brief moment, Goldie's anger was subdued by curiosity. "Why do you call her Miss Magnolia Queen, by the way?"

"She's from a small town in Arkansas called Magnolia, and I think she's already hightailed it back there. I put the fear of God into her when she told me what she did."

"How do you know she left?" asked Ruby.

"I called the next day. The phone was disconnected. I drove by her apartment and peered through the windows. The place was empty. I think it's safe to assume she is back with mommy and daddy in Magnolia. As far as Detective Cooper goes, I was quite candid with him. He asked my whereabouts on the Fourth. I told him the three of us were at my house having a barbecue, which my neighbors would be able to verify. I'm not sure at this point whether he checked with them or not."

Ruby was battling an annoying fly with her left hand. "When he showed up at my place, after badgering me for what seemed forever, he then wanted to search the place. I told him 'Hell, no.' Said he would need to come back with a warrant."

"Why did you do that, Ruby? That makes you look suspicious. I told him to go ahead and search the entire place. Don't worry — I packed all the evidence back up in the suitcase and threw it in the Moyle's garage. I glared at Cooper when he started rummaging through my drawers, sifting through my bras and panties. He was so embarrassed when he saw me watching him, he gave up the search."

Goldie chuckled. "Yeah, I let him search my place too. Of course, it was easy for me — I didn't have anything to hide. I just sat and watched TV, while he feverishly searched for something — anything. Even so, it was kind of spooky. I've been doing a fair amount of thinking," Goldie continued, making her segue into the next topic of conversation. "I was hoping the two of you could help me out with something."

"Goes without saying," said Ruby.

"Sure, Honey. Anything," added Satin.

"Well, I know we're just starting out with the new venture, and my role was to oversee all the girls ... I guess what I'm trying to say is, can you cover for me for a couple of weeks? It's probably better for me to remain incognito for a short while, so I decided to kill two birds with one stone. I called Narcanon, like you suggested. I think I am finally ready to check into rehab. This is my chance to start over, and I want to make the most of it. You know what I mean?"

"Fantastic news," Satin shouted, and the three embraced in a group hug.

"We're here for you," Ruby said, as she gently ran her fingers across Goldie's forehead, sweeping the hair out of her eyes. "Satin and I can split the duties. No sweat."

"Yes, we can. But not until you explain why you stopped Cooper from searching your home, Ruby," Satin said, half-jokingly, half-serious. "Don't you think you drew attention to yourself?"

"No. My girls were there, and I couldn't bear for them to witness that. Besides, I thought our plan was to make it tough for the cops."

Satin shrugged, while Goldie came to Ruby's defense. "I guess if we all seemed too willing for our places to be searched, that in and of itself could arouse suspicion. Anyway, forget about the cops. Frankie's funeral is tomorrow — right here, in this cemetery. Should we go? And I guess we'll have to find a new meeting place in the future."

"Absolutely," Satin said adamantly. "We attend the service here tomorrow. Absence would clearly indicate that we have some malice or, at least, indifference toward Frankie. The cops are aware that we knew Frankie for a long time. It would make us all suspect if we were no-shows. And yes, we'll have a new meeting place. It will be at Frankie's grave instead of this one."

She saw the disapproving looks on the other girls' faces.

"What? It's perfect," Satin said. "We'll never have to worry about who's going to bring the stupid flowers ever again."

"That's creepy," Goldie said with a shudder. "I mean, I don't want to talk about how to get away with Frankie's murder while sitting by his grave. What do you think, Ruby?"

"Actually, it's probably a moot point. Once we have the business up and running, I don't think there will be a need for wig meetings. We can probably put them to rest, like we did with Frankie. We'll have our office, where we can discuss whatever we want, whenever we want. Speaking of which … Satin, when do you think we should start calling the girls and the clients?"

Satin lit another cigarette. "As soon as the funeral service is over tomorrow, we can start with the calls. It will be interesting to see who attends the service and who doesn't. Goldie, when do you plan on checking into rehab?"

Goldie cast her eyes downward. "Well, if it is OK with you, since the service is tomorrow, I would just as soon as check in the day after — on Monday. Before I get cold feet, I guess."

Ruby and Satin put their arms around her.

"You want one of us to drive you there?" asked Satin.

"We'll both take you," Ruby said, before Goldie had a chance to respond. "That way we'll make sure you get checked in properly, and we can check the place out, too. We want to make sure you're in a place where you'll be taken care of."

Goldie smiled. "No one has better friends than I do. Thanks. I honestly don't know how I can ever repay you."

There was a moment of silence before Satin changed the subject. "I've been thinking of names for the new company. So far I've come up with Class Act, Top of the Line, Vegas Best, and Discreetly Yours."

"Those are all good," said Goldie. "I thought of one too: Fifi's Babes."

"Fifi's Babes?" Ruby shot back. "Who the hell is Fifi?"

"It's not so much a who. I was thinking of Fifi's as in Formerly Frankie's Babes. Remember how he forever called all of us that? 'Babes ...' Ugh, I absolutely hated it."

Ruby shook her head. "Sorry, Goldie. Fifi's Babes doesn't do it for me. Other than the clients and the girls, I don't want any connection with Frankie. And I certainly don't want to be reminded of how he called us his 'babes.' I cringe when I think of it. I like Discreetly Yours."

"Me too," Satin said. "That's my favorite one, and so far, it's in the lead with two votes."

"Then count me in," Goldie grumbled. "Discreetly Yours it is, by unanimous decision."

"Great," said Satin. "I'll complete the paperwork online tomorrow. We can sign and make it official on Monday, when we take Goldie to the rehab center." She paused for a moment and then continued, "You know, I think we can make this business a huge success. What do you both plan on doing with your newfound wealth?"

The silence nearly created a vacuum as Ruby and Goldie became completely lost in thought.

Ruby was the first one to snap back into reality. "I'm putting it all toward my girls' education. They'll be able to attend any college they choose. Nothing is more important to me than Maria and Gabby. Nothing. My precious girls, and their happiness is all that matters."

Goldie felt her eyes welling up, so she squinted and looked up toward the sky. "I don't really know," she said. "If I survive Narcanon, then maybe … maybe sometime down the road … maybe I will open my own rehab center." She chuckled at the stunned looks on Satin and Ruby's faces. "I'm serious, you guys. I plan on beating this habit. It's controlled my life for far too long. I think I kind of lost my self-respect somewhere along the way. You know, it wasn't until the two of you asked me to be part of the operation that I actually thought I was worth something to somebody — to anybody." She had a wistful look on her face. "I'd like to give something back. Assuming, of course, I'm not facing a lifetime behind bars."

Satin gave Goldie a gentle hug around the shoulder.

"You're not going down for this, Goldie. Don't worry. I've thought it through. I have insurance policies in place to make sure you're safe. Remember — I've seen Frankie's client list. Don't think for one minute I'll be afraid to use it."

Ruby chimed in. "And don't worry about rehab, either," Ruby said. "You'll get through it. You will. You've got guts, grit, and determination. I've always admired that about you. You're a survivor — it's just a natural instinct for you."

Goldie smiled. "Thank you. Both of you. I mean it. But, enough about me. What about you, Satin? What will you do?"

"I plan on putting in about five years. You can then either buy me out, or we'll sell the business. I want to travel, see the world, go on luxurious cruises. And then, believe it or not, I'd actually like to settle down and get married."

"Are you kidding?" Ruby asked. "How would you explain your life? It's not something any man can overlook."

"I'm not looking for just any man, Ruby. I am looking for that one special man. A knight in shining armor to sweep me off my feet. He's out there. I know he is."

It was Goldie's turn to give Satin a hug. "Hey, you go girl. You're a catch for any man — I hope you manage to reel in the one who deserves you. And, Ruby your daughters are so lucky. You're an amazing mom. But don't forget, your girls want you to be happy too, so don't feel bad if you do something for yourself. Anyway," Goldie continued, "it's time to get going. I've got an appointment with Harvey. Let's see what kind of tricks he wants me to pull out of the hat this time."

They all stood up to leave.

"Well, do you want to carpool to the service tomorrow?" Satin asked. "Remember, I already ordered the floral spray and put all of our names on it. Hopefully, the florist does a better job than you did today, Goldie."

"Hey, knock it off," Goldie chided. "I told you I did the best I could with the flowers."

"I know, I know," Satin said between giggles. "I'm just kidding."

"You're on to something, though," Goldie said. "We're safer together. Ruby, I'll pick you up at one-fifteen tomorrow, and, Satin, we'll swing by your house right after."

Ruby shuddered. "I can't believe they're having the wake at Frankie's house. I wonder who's going to show up. I mean, does he even have any family? Who's going to conduct the eulogy?"

"I guess we'll find out tomorrow afternoon, won't we?" Satin said.

And just like that, the girls got in their cars and drove off.

CHAPTER 19

"**S**eems like it was only yesterday that we were here," Goldie said with a chuckle, as she drove through the cemetery gates.

"That's because it was," Ruby said, playfully slapping her friend's arm from the passenger seat.

"I know — just trying to lighten the mood a little." Goldie pulled the car to a halt behind a couple of already parked cars.

Satin looked at her watch. "There's still ten minutes. Let's just wait in the car until it's time for the service to start." She looked at the neat rows of chairs lined up under the large oak tree. "It looks like there are still several empty seats."

Ruby reached out to grab Goldie's hand. "You feeling OK?"

Goldie nodded. All three of the girls were leaning forward, squinting their eyes, trying to figure out who was there. It was nearly impossible, since all they could see were the backs of the chairs scattered with a few heads.

Satin looked at her watch again. "All right, girls. It's time."

They walked across the lawn, carefully avoiding the headstones in their path, and headed directly for the back row.

"That's our spray — front and center," Satin whispered. "It's the biggest one."

"It's beautiful, Satin, but it's way more than Frankie deserves," Goldie replied, her voice barely audible. "We'll settle up after the service. Can you believe all the chairs here?" Goldie continued, her lips still moving as she counted silently. "They set up six rows of ten seats. Did they honestly expect sixty people to come and pay their respects to Frankie?"

"Never mind the number of seats," Ruby said. "What the hell is Detective Cooper doing here?"

Just then, the minister walked up and stood behind the hollow area where the coffin would be lowered. "Will you please all rise?"

The congregation stood up. The minister proceeded through what seemed to be an endless ceremony before encouraging others to share their memories of Frankie and say their goodbyes. It was no surprise that no one stood to speak.

"Thank, God," Satin said. "I didn't think he'd ever finish."

Before they could be waylaid by anyone, Satin, Ruby, and Goldie, headed back across the manicured lawn

"First service I've ever attended and didn't need tissues," Goldie said.

"Anyone notice how many of Frankie's girls were there?" Satin asked when they got in the car. "And how Pearl was conspicuous by her absence?"

"Yeah, I noticed that too," said Ruby. "I also noticed only two men were there- Detective Cooper and the guy sitting next to him. I'm assuming that's his associate. And who was that woman in the front row, seated by herself?"

Satin lit a cigarette. "Who knows? Maybe it was his housekeeper. Anyway, that service dragged on far longer than I thought possible. I don't want to go to Frankie's house for the after-party, but I know we should. What say both of you that we just stay there for the bare minimum of time?"

"Agreed," Ruby said.

As the car pulled up outside of Frankie's house, Goldie looked through the gate. "This brings back so many god-awful memories, I don't even know if I can go in."

"You can, and you must," Ruby insisted.

"Ruby's right. You need closure, Goldie, and this will give it to you. Plus, we all need to sign the condolence book when we get inside, too."

The three headed up the driveway and entered through the open front door.

"Looks like we're the first to arrive," Satin said. She picked up the pen and signed her name in the otherwise blank condolence book.

"Thank you for coming," said a lady crossing the room. "My name is Julia. I'm a friend of Frankie's sister."

Satin's eyes grew wide. "I didn't know he had a sister."

"Oh, yes," Julia replied. "Her name is Carol. We live in Portland, Oregon. We flew in yesterday morning. Carol should be here shortly." She looked at the three ladies. It was uncomfortably quiet.

"How was the service?" Julia asked, to break the silence. "Oh, here comes Carol now, along with what looks like a number of guests." She excused herself and left.

"This is spooky," Goldie said. "Look at all these photos of Frankie — they're everywhere. It looks like a Frank Sinatra museum."

Ruby was looking around the room, taking it all in — the walls, the tabletops, the carpet. She recounted her last meeting with Frankie in this very room. "I agree," she said. "Very creepy."

Satin poured herself some coffee and helped herself to a plate of hors d'oeuvres. "Let's go out into the garden. We can extend our sympathies to Carol later."

They seated themselves at a table in the gazebo. It wasn't long before they were approached by a visitor.

"Hi, I'm Frank's sister, Carol. May I ask if you are the three ladies who purchased that beautiful spray for my brother?"

Satin was surprised. "Why, yes. How did you know?" She recognized Carol. She was the woman sitting in the front row at the cemetery. *She's much older than Frankie. Boy, don't see any family resemblance. Very matronly looking, but a very kind face.*

Carol shrugged. "Just a hunch. It had three names on it. Looking around the room, I see people in pairs and groups, but here you are, just the three of you, all by yourselves. Seemed kind of obvious." She gave a wan smile, and Satin stepped forward to give her a hug. "So very sorry for your loss, Carol. I'm sure you will miss Frankie terribly."

"I've never heard him called that before," Carol said between sniffles, as she fought the wind, trying to keep her wispy gray hairs out of her face. "What a sweet term of endearment."

Ruby couldn't imagine Frankie being related to this seemingly pleasant and simple woman. She, too, leaned forward and hugged Carol. "My condolences."

"I'm sure you will miss your brother very much," Goldie said with an extended hand. *No way can I hug any relative of the crumb who treated me so badly. Funeral service or no funeral service.*

"Actually, we were not that close. After Frank moved to Las Vegas, I heard very little from him. I used to write, of course, but he never responded — not even on my birthday or for Christmas. I always wanted a better relationship, but it wasn't meant to be."

Goldie held her tongue. *Trust me, you really didn't want a better relationship with him; you really didn't.*

Ruby tried to change the subject. "How long do you plan on staying in town? Your friend Julie said you arrived yesterday."

"Hopefully, just a few days. We just need to sort out a few of Frank's things. It shouldn't take that long."

"Carol," Julia yelled from the house, "I need you."

"Oh, excuse me, I'm sorry. It was so lovely to meet you, and thanks again for sending such a magnificent spray to the service."

No sooner had Carol disappeared inside the house when Detective Cooper and his presumed cohort headed toward them.

"Why is it that every detective looks like Columbo?" Satin asked. "Here we are, in the middle of summer, scorching heat, and they're both wearing raincoats — hands in their pockets, typical swagger — the real-life personification of the stereotypical TV sleuths. Anyway, let me do the talking."

"Good afternoon, ladies. I must say, I'm surprised to see you three here today."

"I can't imagine why, Detective Cooper," Satin said. "We've known Frankie for a long time. The real surprise is why you and your gentleman friend were at the cemetery. And why you've chosen to show up here."

"Just routine, Ma'am. Just routine. This is Officer Len Tyler. He's my assistant on this case."

"What case?" asked Satin, feigning ignorance.

"You know what I'm talking about. And as it happens, I have a few questions for all of you, so I'm glad you're all here."

Satin stood up and picked up her empty plate and cup and saucer. "Well, as it happens, Detective Cooper, you have very bad timing." She gathered her things and stood up. "We carpooled, and Goldie here needs to get back to pack."

"That's no problem, Officer Tyler can run you both home later."

"Thanks for the offer, but we'll have to take a rain check," Satin said. "We're going to help Goldie pack. Why don't you tell them where you're going, Goldie?"

Goldie was caught off guard. She fumbled as she grabbed for her purse and cup. When she finally collected herself, she stood up, ready to speak. "Well," she cleared her throat. "Not that it is really any of your business, Detective Cooper, but tomorrow I'm checking into a rehab center. I need to take of some things beforehand, and my friends are going to help me."

The detective looked at Ruby. "And who's looking after your daughters, while you're looking after your friend?"

"That is *definitely* none of your business, Detective Cooper," Ruby shot back.

As the three headed toward the house, the detective asked one final question.

"Any of you know where I can find Patty-Ann Stratford, more commonly known as Pearl?"

Satin stopped and turned around. "Aren't you the detective?" she asked. Without waiting for a reply, she smiled at the two men, and led the way inside.

Officer Tyler looked at his superior. "What are you thinking, Mark?"

"They're like the three musketeers," he replied. "They have an iron-clad alibi with each other when the murder took place. They arrived at the cemetery together. They sent a funeral spray together. They signed the condolence book here together. Everyone is mingling inside, and they're out here together. Now, they're leaving together. My hunch is that one of them — which means all of them — is involved in this murder. I've been a detective for 35 years, and I've never been wrong about a hunch. I pray this will not be the first time. But if any one of them did do it … make no mistake, I will see to it that they are nailed to the mast."

PART 2
DISCREETLY YOURS

CHAPTER 20

W
ith Satin, Ruby, and Goldie at the helm, Discreetly Yours had been running smoothly for four months. Business was good. Satin followed a strict vetting process when it came to accepting new clientele, Ruby was adept at handling the finances, and Goldie kept the escorts in line.

From her office on the 18th floor, Satin had a clear view of the Strip. Swiveling back and forth in her chair, she looked out her window, hypnotized by the flashing lights.

Would you believe it? she thought, her hands toying with her blond locks. *Probably something I should have done years ago. But, then again, I wouldn't be so fortunate if I weren't working with such amazing partners. Ruby and Goldie — they really are the two most trusted souls I know. It's a perfect combination. We run this place like a well-oiled machine.* She pivoted her chair around completely, appreciating the plush décor and eclectic pieces of art on the walls. *Ruby certainly has an eye for design.*

After basking in the glory of her success, she opened her laptop to review the client list. She was proud of her filing system— clients could be sorted alphabetically or by profession, preferences, age, frequency of dates, and price range. When she opened up the 'staff' files, she couldn't help but laugh. *Well, that's Goldie. As long as she can make sense of her system, I guess that's all that matters. Besides, I never hear any complaints from the crew.*

Out of curiosity, she opened up a few of the files, chuckling quietly as she read Goldie's very matter-of-factly stated notes about the girls, including their do's and don'ts. The only thing left to check was the books, which, as expected, were in impeccable condition. *How gratifying to see such a healthy bank balance, with plenty of cash in both the checking and the savings account. What a nice little nest egg. We should be able to have some nice profit sharing at the end of the year.*

She jumped as the phone rang. "Discreetly Yours..." she answered.

"Hello."

"What? Why are you calling on the business line? Let me call you back on my cellphone."

"No — I'll call you back on your cell. I'm calling from another office. I just wanted to make sure I got to speak to you."

Whenever Judge Richard called, as he had done several times since they first met, it threw her mind in a turmoil. The phone rang again. This time, it was her cellphone.

"Well, hello, Judge."

"Hello. I'm surprised — and flattered — that you recognized my voice."

"All part of the job. Are you calling to wish me a Happy Thanksgiving?"

"No, I was actually calling to ask you to spend Thanksgiving with me."

Satin fell silent. When Richard repeated the question, she rubbed her forehead and took a deep breath. "Why aren't you spending it with your family?"

"Deidre didn't want to come home from college, so my wife went there. They'll both be here for Christmas."

"How come you always say 'my wife' instead of using her name?"

"Do I? I'd never noticed. Her name is Janice."

"Why didn't you go with Janice to see Deidre?"

"I have a huge caseload and decided it would be a good time to catch up on the paperwork. But with the courthouse being closed on Thanksgiving Day, I think I'm entitled to the day off, too."

"And you don't want to spend it alone, right?"

"Satin, you know it's more than that. You remember the night of the fundraiser. You have to admit — we had a bond, a connection."

"Yes, but you have to remember that I'm no longer in the business. I'm running it now, and I really want to keep it that way." But Satin's mind traveled back to that evening. She remembered it distinctly. It was a night she had thought about often — one she would never forget. And though she hated to admit it, it was more than just a physical attraction. "To be quite honest, I enjoy my life now. I'm happier and more content than I've ever been."

"You can't be serious. You're happy running an escort agency?"

"It is not just an escort agency, Judge. It is *the* premier escort agency in Las Vegas. We're the best."

"Don't I know it?" He chuckled.

"My partners and I have worked very hard to make it that way."

"You're avoiding my question, Satin."

"I'm not. I'm just trying to be practical. Where would we meet, even if I agreed?"

"Well, I was thinking you could come over to my house."

"That's crazy!"

"What? I'm a pretty good chef. I can whip up a Thanksgiving dinner."

"It's not that — I don't want to spend Thanksgiving at your house, where you live with your wife. Besides, she would know as soon as she came back. Women can sense these things."

"There are plenty of places we can go."

The business phone started ringing. It was Ruby.

"Let me call you back," Satin said reluctantly. She simultaneously hung up her cell and picked up the office phone. "Hi, Ruby. What's up?"

"You need to get here — to my house. Now."

Satin sensed a certain frantic tone in Ruby's voice. "What's the matter?" she asked.

"I need you here, now. It's urgent. It's about the wigs."

They closed the doors on their wig meetings when they opened the doors to their office, but Satin picked up on the signal.

"I'll be right there. Should I call Goldie?"

"No. It's about Goldie. Just get over here ASAP."

Satin forwarded the calls to her cell, locked the offices, and headed to Ruby's house.

What's happened to Goldie? she wondered as both her mind and the car raced along the freeway. *Please God, don't tell me she's had a relapse. She's been doing so well since rehab. Best thing that happened to her. Wow, I hope it's nothing worse. What if she's been in an accident or something?* Satin caught a glimpse of the speedometer and immediately slowed.

She pulled up in front of Ruby's house. Another car was parked there, almost blocking the driveway. Before she could open her door, Ruby ran out and hopped in the passenger side of the car.

"What is it, Ruby? What's wrong?"

Ruby was ashen-faced. "It's Goldie. She's just been arrested. She called me to see if we can bail her out."

CHAPTER 21

atin sped off like a maniac. "Where am I going? The prison or the detention center?"

Ruby strapped herself in securely and muttered a *Hail Mary* under her breath.

"The detention center—at thirty-three hundred, Spencer. Goldie called me on my cell, but I had to set up an account with the phone company to accept the collect call. All she said was to come and get her out. I told her we'd be right there, and she hung up. I think the calls are recorded, so I suspect that's why she kept it to a minimum."

Like a stunt driver, Satin flew by the other drivers on the road, one hand on the wheel, the other hand typing the address in her GPS.

"Good God. Well, what exactly was she arrested for? She hasn't gone back to drugs again, has she?"

"Who the hell knows," Ruby said, becoming more nervous with each passing second. "I hope not. I've been so proud of her since she went to that rehab center. They did wonders for her."

"I know. I feel the same way. I don't know why I said that. It's just … her arrest can't have anything to do with Frankie. Not after all of this time. I mean, it's been months. There's no way they're still collecting new evidence at this stage … right?"

"I guess we're about to find out."

"I don't know, Ruby, I have a bad feeling about this. What if she was arrested for the murder? Do you think it's a good idea for both of us to go into the detention center?"

"What do you mean? You're not thinking of hanging Goldie out to dry, are you?"

"Of course not. But I wouldn't put anything past that weasel of a detective and his moronic sidekick. I bet he's already found out who she called. He will definitely check the sign-in book to see who visited."

"You're right. So, what do you suggest we do?"

Satin thought for a minute. "Goldie is obviously going to need bail."

"Yeah — how are we going to come up with the money?" Ruby asked.

"We'll take it from the business if we have to. It'll be returned."

"If she's in for murder, she's going to need more money than we have. Hopefully, that's not the case. Otherwise, I'll have to speak to Daddy Warbucks."

"Are you still seeing that guy? I thought the whole purpose of running the business was so that we don't have to deal with these guys anymore."

"I don't see him anymore, but we still talk. He is one of our customers, you know, and I want to keep it that way. I love spending the evenings with my girls -helping them with their homework, reading to them, putting them to bed. And I can't do that without paying customers like him."

Satin smiled at Ruby's contentment. "Who's looking after the girls this evening? Margaret?"

"Yes. She came at a moment's notice, God love her. She looked so worried and so frantic when I told her I had an emergency."

"How much did you tell her about Frankie and Goldie?"

"Nothing. She is such a worrywart. The less she knows, the better."

When they pulled up to the detention center, it was completely dark, except for a sliver of light emanating from the moon. Satin drove slowly as they looked for the entrance. "My God," she said. For a moment, she just sat there - staring. If the building itself didn't give off a creepy enough vibe, the high security gate surrounding it sure did. "I bet Colditz POW camp during World War II didn't even look this foreboding."

"Yeah," Ruby said. "I guess visiting hours are over."

They both laughed nervously.

"As we were coming along Spencer, I saw a light. I'm going to drive back around and see what it is." She stopped just outside the window. Though the light was on, it appeared no one was inside. The street was empty, not a car in sight. "Are you OK waiting in the car?"

Ruby chuckled. "I'm probably safer here than you are in there. But, anyway, don't worry. I have Mace."

Satin parked the car and made her way to the dimly lit window. She felt surrounded by a cold and sinister atmosphere. It was quiet aside from the incessant barking of a dog in the distance.

On the other side of the glass was a reception area, which consisted of one small cubicle. The middle-aged dour-looking woman who appeared to be working, judging by her uniform, never looked up from her computer. "Can I help you?" she asked.

"I'm trying to bail someone out," Satin shouted through the window pane.

"Name?" The response was monotone.

"Her name is Gloriana Berelowitz."

"Do you have an appointment?"

"No, I wasn't aware I needed one."

The attendant continued tapping the computer. "Berelowitz is here on a murder charge. No bail has been set yet."

Satin was stunned. "Well, can I see her?"

"No, Ma'am. I can't help you."

"She must be terrified. Is there anything you can do?"

"We all have problems, Ma'am. Besides, it's time for my break."

A new attendant walked in, and Satin was relieved when she recognized her as someone who had worked for Frankie for a short time a few years back. "Ashley, it's great to see you," she said. "But what in the world are you doing here?"

Ashley smiled and came over to the window, clicking the switch for the two-way microphone. "I might ask you the same question. Anyway, it's good to see you, Satin. And for the record, my name is Shirley. Ashley was just my working name. And this sure the heck beats working for Frankie — even if the money is the pits."

Satin was confused. "But at least you made good pay with Frankie. What do you get out of working here?"

Ashley shrugged. "I get retirement and good health benefits. But you know, I get to help people when they come in here. So many of them are distraught. You know what I mean? Their loved ones are behind that door." She nodded at the large metal door behind her. "Sometimes, I calm them down. I take away their fears and settle their nerves. It's particularly tough for the mothers who have to visit their kids here — especially the elderly moms."

"Well you certainly have a different outlook than your predecessor."

"Jessie? You had problems with Jessie?"

"Well, let's say she certainly didn't help, and I'll just leave it at that. Do you remember Goldie?"

Ashley nodded. "How can anyone forget Goldie?"

"She's in here. And I need to see her. I need to get her bail sorted out, so she can get out of here."

"What's her real name?"

"Gloriana Berelowitz."

Ashley returned to the desk and typed her name into the computer.

"Sorry, Honey. You don't have an appointment. You can't see anyone without it being cleared. I assumed she was here for drugs, but I see she's here for murder. The best thing you can do is get her a lawyer. Pronto. She needs to get bail through a judge. There's usually a bail sentencing of at least one hundred thousand dollars."

Satin almost choked. "You're kidding me, right?"

Ashley shook her head.

"Is there any way I can see her for a minute? Just for one lousy minute?"

Ashley shook her head again.

"You can't. It's all recorded on video. What I can do for you, though, is tell her you were here."

"Can you give her a message?"

"Sure."

"Great. Could you tell her to call Ruby? I'm going to get her a top-notch attorney and see about a judge. Just please let her know that we're dealing with it, and we'll have someone here first thing tomorrow. Would love to stay and chat, but I must go, so I can get working on it."

"Sure thing, Honey, but be careful — the calls are recorded. I'm really glad I ran into you — maybe we can meet up for lunch sometime and you can fill me in?"

"I'd love that. Thanks for helping Goldie. You're a star." Satin hurried down the steps and back to the car. She filled Ruby in on everything.

"I'll call Daddy Warbucks as soon as I get home," said Ruby, muttering another *Hail Mary* as Satin floored it again.

"Great. I'll go to the office to see which powerful attorneys we have on our roster. I'm sure we can get at least one of them to do some pro bono work."

"Good idea. We'll get her out of there." Ruby's cell phone rang and she looked at the number. "Hang on, it's Goldie. Let me take the call."

"Well, at least Ashley kept her word and got the message to Goldie. And be careful what you say. All the calls are recorded."

CHAPTER 22

"**W**here the hell are you?" Goldie yelled frantically into the phone. "You were supposed to be here to get me out of this hellhole."

"Calm down, Honey. It's not that simple. Satin and I can't do anything until tomorrow morning."

"For Christ's sake. I can't spend the night here. You've no idea what it's like. It stinks, and you should see some of the crud lurking around. It's giving me the creeps."

"Just hang tight. We'll get you out first thing in the morning. You can count on us. I Promise." Ruby hung up.

"Since the bail is likely to be at least one hundred thousand dollars, how much do you think you can squeeze from Daddy Warbucks?" Satin asked.

"I don't know. He could pay the entire amount, and it wouldn't make a dent in his bank account. I'm going to have to work at it though. Sometimes, he can be pretty darn cheap."

"Aren't they all?" grumbled Satin, as she pulled into Ruby's driveway. "I'm going to head back to the office, see what I can do about getting Goldie in front of a friendly judge, and try to line up a good attorney. When you know how much you can get from Daddy Warbucks, text me. Just put in the number, don't mention what for. I'll deal with the rest."

"You bet. I'll tell Margaret I have a headache, and she'll leave early. Hopefully, the girls are asleep. I'll jump right on it. We'll chat later, OK?"

Satin nodded. She waited until Ruby was inside before driving away.

When Ruby stepped inside, she noticed the harried look on her sister's face. Margaret rose from the couch, where she'd been watching the television. "Is everything alright?" she asked as they hugged.

"Everything is fine," Ruby assured her. "I've just got a splitting headache. I'm going to take a pill and go straight to bed. Do you mind?"

"Not at all. The girls are asleep. I read them a story. They were both in dream world before I got half way through it," she chuckled. "Let me get my purse, so you can get some sleep. Hopefully your headache will be gone by tomorrow."

Ruby sat down on the couch and removed her shoes. "You're a Godsend, Margaret. What would I do without you?"

From behind the couch, Margaret leaned forward and kissed her sister. "Goodnight," she said, closing the front door behind her.

"Give my love to Dave," Ruby shouted after her.

As soon as Margaret had departed, Ruby went quietly upstairs to see her girls. She smiled upon seeing both of them sleeping so peacefully, the moonlight shining brightly in their room. She tiptoed softly down the stairs and poured herself a vodka and tonic. She turned the volume on the TV down and stretched out on the couch.

Let's see what I can do with my friendly local banker in Spanish Trails, she mused, as she dialed his number.

"I thought I told you never to call me on this number unless it was an emergency."

"Well, that's a fine way to treat someone who's been so good to you over the years," she teased. "But this *is* an emergency"

"Can it wait for a few hours? It's poker night. The guys are all here," he whispered.

"If it could wait, Nigel, it wouldn't be an emergency, now would it?"

"Hold on a moment." He yelled out to his company, "Hey guys. Deal me out the next hand. I need to take care of something."

Ruby heard him close the door.

"OK, Honey. You have my undivided attention. What is it that is so important it couldn't wait?"

Ruby decided to go straight for the jugular. *I can always negotiate down, but never up,* she thought. "I need one hundred thousand dollars. A colleague of mine is in serious trouble."

"You're kidding me, right? Where do you think I can get that kind of money?" He laughed nervously.

"I need it tomorrow. For you, that kind of money is just a rounding figure on your tax return. You wouldn't even miss it."

Nigel thought for a moment. "What did your friend do? That's a lot of cash."

"It's bail money. She's been accused of murder."

"Murder, huh? Did she do it?"

"Believe me, Nigel, the less I say, the better."

There was a silence on the line. "I miss you, Ruby."

"You're well taken care of. I know who sees you now."

"None of them are same, Honey. Not even in the same class."

Ruby thought he sounded a little wistful and melancholy. "I'd love to reminisce, Nigel, but I don't have the time for a trip down memory lane. I've got to get this money together before tomorrow morning. You know you'll get it back."

"Tell you what. I'll give you fifty-grand. But keep me out of this whole thing, OK? Swing by the bank first thing tomorrow. I'll have it for you in cash."

"You're the best, Nigel. I owe you one."

"You owe me fifty. Now let me get back to my game."

"Thank you, Nigel. I mean it."

They hung up. She took a swig of her drink and realized she hadn't had anything to eat. She headed to the fridge and found a couple of chicken wings and some leftover coleslaw. *I've worked all my life, and this is what I have for my dinner? Leftover chicken and coleslaw? Oh well, at least Satin should be happy with what I've accomplished. Which reminds me ...*

She grabbed her phone, and texted Satin. She typed in 'fifty' and hit send.

Back in the office, Satin braced herself for what she knew would be a grueling evening. She went to the wet bar, mixed herself a Manhattan, kicked off her shoes, and got comfortable behind the desk. As she scrolled through all the clients on the computer listed as attorneys, some of the names sounded vaguely familiar. But she wanted the best for Goldie, and there was one name in particular that caught her eye. She took a long sip of her drink and dialed the number. Expecting her call to go straight to voicemail, she was a little taken aback when someone actually answered. *Don't be nervous now. Remember, you have the upper hand. Just cut to the point.*

"I'm calling for Mr. Lamont."

"Brett Lamont speaking. Who is this?"

"Mr. Lamont, I need to retain your services for a friend of mine who is currently in the Las Vegas Detention Center."

"Who is this, and how did you get my number?"

"The details aren't important. This case requires immediate attention."

"Call my office in the morning then, and we'll set up an appointment for next week."

Undeterred, Satin continued, even though he sounded irritated. She knew she would win in the end. "It can't wait until next week. My friend is on a murder charge. She was arrested today. I need to get her out on bail immediately."

"That's not possible. It will take a few days for the paperwork to go through the system. And that's only if the judge is so inclined to even grant bail at the arraignment. In which case, chances are it will be a minimum of a hundred thousand dollars. And, for the last time, who is this?"

"The bail money is secured. And don't worry, the judge will grant her bail. I can guarantee you that."

"How can you be so sure? I don't think I can help in this case. But if you call my office tomorrow, I will refer you to a good attorney — under one condition, that is. You have to tell me who you are."

"I believe I already have a good attorney — you. It seems we have a mutual friend in common. Her name is Pearl."

There was a lengthy pause before the lawyer responded. "What do you know about Pearl?"

With no time to waste, Satin played her trump card right away. "Enough to know she was underage when you were seeing her."

"What? I never knew she was underage. That's impossible. Where is she now? She's not the one up for murder, is she?"

It was exactly the response Satin was hoping to elicit. *I've got him exactly where I want him,* she thought. "Never mind where Pearl is. She's not the one up for murder, but I can certainly get her back here at a moment's notice. She can only spell trouble for you, Mr. Lamont, if word gets out. Now, will you take my case?"

"Even if I did, it's impossible to get an arraignment for tomorrow."

"Come on now, nothing is impossible." Satin was beginning to enjoy the conversation. Drink in hand, she walked from the desk to the sofa and laid down, resting her tired feet on the cushions.

"How do you know what judge you will get, and how can you be so sure he or she will grant bail?"

"You just get my friend to the arraignment, and I'll take care of the rest. With all your contacts at the courthouse, I'm sure you can call in a few favors."

"Wait. I still don't know who you are and who will pay the costs."

Satin detected he was nervous, but sensed he'd be perfect in the courtroom. "My name's Serena Young. I'll be at the court tomorrow to introduce myself. The name of my friend with the murder charge is Gloriana Berelowitz. Now if you'll forgive me, I have a few more phone calls to make. It has been a pleasure talking to you, Mr. Lamont. See you tomorrow. I know you won't let me down." She hung up, convinced he would do whatever it took to get Goldie's arraignment.

She looked at her phone and saw Ruby's text message. "Well done," she texted back. "We're good. Hired someone to take care of the other." *Now let me see what my good friend, Judge Richard, can do for me.* She mixed herself another drink and dialed his number.

Richard was watching TV with his wife when his phone rang. He recognized Satin's phone number and quickly answered. "Hold on," he said, as he removed his arm from around his wife. "I'll be just a few minutes, Honey. It's business."

What a liar, Satin thought. She was surprised at the abrupt tone in his voice when he turned back to her.

"What are you thinking, calling me at home?"

"I have an emergency. I need you to resolve it."

"Can't it wait until tomorrow?"

"No, it can't. I have a friend at the Las Vegas Detention Center. She is being arraigned tomorrow. I need the judge to approve bail."

"This can't be dealt with tonight over a phone call. I need some help here. Who's the judge? Who's representing the DA's office? Who's defending your friend? What time is the arraignment? I need to know more details, and I'm not sure if you have them. There are procedures to follow."

Satin rolled her eyes. "I don't know. I haven't a clue as to the answers to any of your questions, except the attorney I've hired. But what difference does it make? I need you to make sure my friend gets out."

"What? You're asking me, a judge, to thwart the judicial system?"

"It happens all the time. You know that."

"Not by me it doesn't."

Satin sat up on the sofa. "Well, there's a first for everything. I'm calling in a favor, Richard."

There was a long silence. Finally, he responded. "You realize you're asking me to betray an oath."

She was not in the mood for any of his pouts. "You've already betrayed an oath ... to your wife."

"That's cold." He paused for a moment. "Is this what has become of our relationship?"

"Relationship? What relationship? Richard, I'm very serious here. I'm talking about survival. Unless you take care of this, there could be very serious ramifications for a lot of people in this city."

"How's that? What crime has your friend committed?"

"Her name is Gloriana Berelowitz. She's being charged with murder."

He was stunned. "I can't get involved with that."

"Richard, I am deadly serious. If this isn't dealt with, many people are going to get hurt. Lives will be ruined."

"Are you blackmailing me?"

"No, Richard. I'm asking a favor. If everyone cooperates, things will smooth over."

"I'm not sure if it's even in my jurisdiction. I can't help."

"Yes, you can. You know all the judges. That's about as close a circle there is. You can check the court docket tomorrow and speak to the assigned judge."

Richard thought a little. "I'll see what I can do," he said quietly.

"Thank you. I'm counting on you, so please don't let me down."

"I'm not making any promises."

"It had better be a promise, you hear? We're talking about survival. And make sure whoever presides grants bail at no more than one hundred thousand dollars. That's all we have. Good night, Richard." She hung up. *Damn, I'm good,* she thought, feeling very smug. She lit a cigarette, finished her Manhattan, and texted Ruby one more time. "We're good for tomorrow, but might be an idea to wear a wig."

Richard wiped the beads of sweat from his brow. The threatening tone in Satin's voice caused him to worry where his intervention might lead if she had damning evidence on their tryst. He was concerned about the consequences — for himself and others — in the event it was disclosed.

CHAPTER 23

"Bail for the defendant granted in the amount of one hundred thousand dollars. Court stands adjourned." The judge slammed the gavel on the table and rose from his desk.

"Thank you, Your Honor," Brett said.

Satin and Ruby were seated at the back of the courtroom. They hugged each other when they heard the judge's decision. They watched as the attorney conferred with Goldie.

Satin grabbed her purse. "C'mon, let's wait in the lobby. We have some business to discuss with the attorney."

Ruby followed her out. "Shouldn't we go and post Goldie's bail first? It was heart-wrenching to see her in shackles today."

They both sat down on the nearby bench.

"I agree. But we can't blow this. We need to get Goldie out, which means we need to get Lamont on board for the entire case. I checked him out, and I'll tell you what — this guy's got baggage. But he has a great record as a defense attorney."

The doors to the courtroom opened, and Brett strode out, briefcase in hand. The two women immediately stood.

"Mr. Lamont, I'm Serena Young, and this is my friend, Rhonda Smallwell." Satin gestured to Ruby before extending her hand to the lawyer.

Brett ignored it. He glared at her through his black-rimmed glasses. "Well, you got what you want. Your friend is out on bail. I hope you're happy." He turned and headed toward the exit of the court.

Satin and Ruby followed him. "But, Mr. Lamont, we're not finished yet."

He stopped, turned, and glared at her again, totally ignoring Ruby.

"Oh yes we are, Ms. Young. We're very much finished. You've no idea the hoops and hurdles I had to jump through, not to mention all the favors I had to call in, to make this happen for you. You've already placed me in a very compromising position."

"You put yourself in a compromising position when you engaged the services of Pearl — who, I will remind you, was underage at the time."

The doors of the courtroom opened again, and the prosecuting attorney emerged, her face as black as thunder. *What a frump,* thought Satin, as she watched the middle-aged, plump lady march toward them in her brown tweed suit. "Something stinks here, Brett," she fumed, as if Satin and Ruby were not even there. "I don't know how this got on the court docket today. We were totally unprepared. I don't like it, do you read me? I don't like it. And I will get to the bottom of it. You can stake your life on that." Without waiting for an answer, she stormed out of the courthouse.

The attorney looked at Satin. "You see what I mean? I don't want any part of this. I doubt it's even a winnable case. Find someone else to do your dirty work."

"We do have a winning case, Mr. Lamont, and you're going to win it for us. If you can't beat that battle-axe of a prosecutor, the legal system really is in trouble."

He bristled. "Her name is Madge Williams. She is one very sharp lady who deserves respect. She is one of the most prominent members of the district attorneys' team."

Satin was growing impatient. Her eyes made direct contact with his. "She, and the assistant with her in the courtroom today, are like arsenic and old lace. If you don't take this case, I'll have to see about going to the American Bar Association. You're not the only one who had to go through hoops and hurdles, Mr. Lamont. As you must surely be aware, Gloriana's release was not solely due to your efforts."

After a moment of silence, Brett dipped his hand in the top pocket of his pin-striped suit and removed a business card. He glanced around to make sure no one was watching before handing it to her.

"Be at my office at five-thirty tonight. We'll talk. My advice to you is to get over to the detention center, and post the bail — if you have it."

"Of course we have it. We're heading there right now. Just wanted to conclude our business first." Satin extended her hand for a second time, only to be rebuffed. The attorney looked at both ladies with disdain, and headed to the courthouse doors.

"What an arrogant pig," Ruby noted as she watched him leave. "Are you sure this is the guy we want?"

"Don't worry, Ruby. We'll knock him into place when we meet at his office this evening. I'm not taking that treatment from him, nor are any of us. We took enough of that from Frankie. Brett Lamont will know who is in charge. C'mon, let's carpool to the detention center, and get this bail posted."

"You were masterful with him, Satin. I'm proud of you. Goldie will be, too."

"Goldie will be proud of you as well, Ruby. The way you sweet-talked Daddy Warbucks into giving fifty-grand for her bail. That was awesome!"

The girls raced to fill out the endless stack of paperwork. Then they waited, and waited for what seemed like an eternity before Goldie finally emerged.

Goldie was so overcome with emotion, tears rolled down her cheeks. "I didn't think you guys would be able to make bail. I had visions of being stuck in that hellhole forever. I don't know how you pulled this off, but I'm so glad you did."

Ruby put her arms around her friend as they walked to Satin's car. "Hey, don't you remember? We're the three musketeers. All for one, and one for all."

Satin climbed into her car. "Well, you can thank Ruby for scoring fifty-grand from Daddy Warbucks. The rest, we pulled from the business."

"And Satin managed to pull a few strings to get your case on today's court docket — and to make sure bail would be granted."

Goldie was stunned. "You mean this was all rigged?"

Satin kept looking in her rearview mirror. "In a manner of speaking. I'm going to take a couple of weird turns, just to make sure we're not being followed by that creepy detective. Let's go grab a sandwich and a cup of coffee and catch up."

"A sandwich and coffee? Are you kidding me? I've been in the slammer, for God's sake. I need a juicy steak and a celebration drink." Goldie pulled out a mirror along with a comb from her purse, and ran it through her hair. "I look like hell."

Satin, aware of what lay ahead for all of them, was a little wary. Still, she was not about to deprive Goldie. She smiled at her friend in the back seat. "OK. I know this place on the far side of Henderson. They serve great steaks. It's really dark inside. The bar and restaurant are dimly lit, so hopefully, no one will recognize us. There's a bag on the floor next to you, Goldie, with a wig inside. I suggest you put it on."

"Jeez, I've just combed my hair. Hope it's not like that ghastly one you forced me to wear on the Fourth," Goldie said, fumbling inside the bag.

Ruby lit a cigarette. "It reminds me of the old days. I never thought we'd be doing this wig meeting stuff again."

"Just a precaution," warned Satin. "We can't be too long having a bite. We'll all need to get home and change. Our meeting with the attorney is at five-thirty, and all three of us need to be there. I think we should drive there separately and meet in the lobby. His card says he is on the seventh floor."

"Hey, by the way, where did you find this attorney? He's a bit stiff isn't he?" Goldie asked as she struggled with the wig. "He could easily be mistaken for a secret service agent. Anyhow, why do all three of us have to go? You don't need to involve yourselves, do you?"

"Safety in numbers, Goldie, and we're the three musketeers." Satin said. "We'll fill you in over lunch about how we found this guy." She turned her car onto the freeway and drove toward Henderson.

*****

"Is there anything else you need before I leave tonight?" Brett's secretary asked.

He looked at his watch. It was exactly five o'clock. "Gee, I don't know where the time went today. Just leave the coffeepot on — I'll be working a little late tonight. And if you could bring me the McAllister file, that would be great. Thank you, Marcia."

"Oh, the coffee has been sitting a long time. I'll make a fresh pot for you."

Brett became nervous. The last thing he needed was for his middle-aged and very proper secretary to see an attractive lady arriving in his office. "Oh, please don't trouble yourself, Marcia. I'll be fine. Just run along and don't worry about locking up. I'll take care of that."

"No trouble at all. It'll only take me five minutes." She disappeared from the office only to return a few minutes later. "Coffee's all made, and here's the file you wanted. Don't work too late now." She stood next to him and looked out the window with amazement at the Las Vegas skyline with the dark mountains in the background. "I must say, I never tire of looking at this wonderful view from your office. It always seems so mysterious."

"Thank you. It is a magnificent view, isn't it?" Growing more anxious by the second, he stood up from his desk and gently guided her out of his office.

Oblivious to her boss' behavior, she continued talking. "Now, don't forget to switch the coffee off before you leave. And when you put the file back in the cabinet, please remember to lock it and place the keys in the back of my middle, right-hand drawer."

"Right. Don't worry, Marcia. I'll take care of everything."

He opened the door to the front office and watched until his loyal secretary entered the elevator. He returned to his office, leaving his door open, so he could hear Satin when she arrived.

At precisely five-thirty, he heard the front door open. He was surprised to see three ladies walk through the door.

"I must confess, I was not expecting all three of you, but since you're all here, please step into my office. My secretary has just made some fresh coffee. Would you like some?"

So very matter-of-fact, thought Satin. "I'm fine thank you."

Brett pulled an extra chair up to his desk. "What about you ladies?"

Both Ruby and Goldie shook their heads. Once they were all seated, Satin decided that attack was the best form of defense.

"First, Mr. Lamont. You already know Gloriana. Today, you also met, but did not acknowledge, Ruby. From now on, you will ignore none of us, and you will treat us with respect, as will we with you. Do we understand each other?"

Clasping his hands, and leaning forward on the desk, Brett responded with equal force. "Ms. Young, I am not accustomed to being spoken to in this manner. You clearly do not respect me, and the feeling is mutual. Now, if you're uncomfortable, I'm more than happy to refer you to another attorney. Consider the services rendered in court this morning complimentary."

Satin leaned forward and, adopting the same posture, clasped her hands together. "Mr. Lamont, not only will this morning's services be complimentary, but you will see this case through trial, and it will all be pro bono. We know where Pearl is, and as I mentioned last night, I can have her back here at a moment's notice. Two of us witnessed the prosecutor's observations and comments this morning in the lobby of the courthouse. I'm sure she would love to hear what we have to say about how this case got on today's docket."

"I will not be blackmailed, Ms. Young." His voice was firm and growing louder.

Satin showed perfect equanimity. She pulled out a cigarette from her purse and lit it. It was her way of indicating her level of composure and would not be intimidated by his tone. "And we will not be dismissed by someone who commits statutory rape. We have all the records and the evidence. Furthermore, we know people in high places. Once again, let me remind you, it was I who made sure that bail would be granted today. Of course, you helped," she said, shrugging her shoulders. "But, I clinched it. Now do we have a deal here, or do I have to use alternative methods for a resolution?"

Brett looked down and rolled his thumbs. Finally, leaning back in his chair, he sighed and agreed. "I'm not making any promises," he said. "But let's see what you have. Where do you want to start?"

Satin smiled. "Well, Brett, since we are all going to be working together for the foreseeable future, I think we can start referring to each other on a first name basis. The bottom line is, Gloriana — we call her Goldie — has been accused of murder, which she did not commit. The murder took place on the Fourth of July, and the three of us were having a barbecue at my home."

Brett started scribbling notes on a yellow pad. "Any witnesses?"

"Yes. We were on my front porch. My neighbors were on their porch, too, the entire time. We even had a conversation with them."

Brett looked at Goldie. "Did you know the deceased — Frankie, or whatever his name is?"

It was Goldie's turn to light a cigarette. "We all did. We worked for him."

"Pearl worked for him, too, Brett," Satin added. "Let's just say, we inherited Frankie's records. As you can imagine, there are many interesting names in his files."

Brett realized, for the first time, the gravity and volatility of the situation. He was in a precarious position. Looking at the three women sitting opposite of him, he wondered if he could be at the center of the biggest legal scandal in Nevada history.

CHAPTER 24

Ruby interrupted the attorney's train of thought. "You don't seem to be making many notes, Brett. Isn't it important for you to jot a few things down at least? Or are we being recorded?"

Brett was irritated. "Ladies, if you want me to take this case — and do it pro bono — you need to let me handle it as I see fit. I'm not sure I want to keep detailed notes, nor do I think you want to have your comments recorded. Do we understand each other?"

The ladies looked at each other and nodded. "You're right," Ruby said. "I'm sorry."

"Well, I sure as heck would like to know on what grounds I was arrested," snapped Goldie. "That Columbo-wannabe, Detective Bill Cooper, and his sidekick, Mr. Stiffy, just showed up at my house with an arrest warrant and hauled me off."

Brett frowned. "Don't sell Detective Cooper short. He's one sharp investigator. He normally has something pretty solid that sticks before going to the DA's office. He has pretty good intuition as well."

Satin crossed her legs and pulled at her skirt a little. "Well, his instincts are wrong here, I can assure you. We have cast-iron proof of Goldie's whereabouts."

Brett looked at the attractive ladies, and he almost felt a sense of admiration for them. *I don't believe their story for one second. Cooper's too smart. He's found a loophole in their alibi somewhere. But these ladies are pretty shrewd, too. This is going to be interesting.* "Obviously I don't have any idea of what the detective or the DA's office has. Due to your stunts, as you can imagine, I had no time to talk to Madge Williams. I'll see her tomorrow and find out what she has."

"Does this mean you're going to represent me?" asked Goldie.

"Let me see what they have, and we'll take it from there. In the meantime, apart from the testimony of the three of you, what do we have on our side of the ledger?"

Satin liked the way that sounded and smiled. "My neighbors. They're real nosy. I call them Gladys and Abner Kravitz, after the nosy neighbors in the old TV sitcom *Bewitched.* Their real names are Sheila and Alan Godfrey."

Brett chuckled. *First, Columbo and now the Kravitzes. Wonder what name they'll give to me.*

As if reading his mind, Ruby chimed in. "We're going to call you Perry Mason, since you'll get Goldie an acquittal."

They all laughed, and the tension eased. It was a defining moment.

"Ruby and Goldie carpooled to my house," Satin continued. "When they arrived, Gladys and Abner were peering through the windows, as is their custom. I could see them. I decided to show Ruby and Goldie my garden. As we came to the flower beds near the Kravitzes house, we waved to them. Shortly after that, as we were sitting on the porch having appetizers and drinks, true to form, out came Gladys and Abner to sit on their porch. I yelled over the fence and asked them to join us for the barbecue, but they declined. After our meal, which we had on the outside porch, they were still there, fixated. Goldie even took them over a piece of cake."

Brett scratched his forehead. "Are they prepared to testify on your behalf though?"

"You can subpoena them, can't you?" Satin responded.

"Yes. It just makes life easier if you have friendly witnesses as opposed to hostile ones. Anything else?"

"What more do you need? It was a small, friendly Fourth of July barbecue. Do you expect a gathering of the reincarnation of the Founding Fathers?" Goldie threw her hands in the air, and they all shared another laugh.

"No. I just wanted to make sure I had all the witnesses and all the evidence. Do any of you have any family you would have normally been spending the holiday with?"

"Just me," Ruby said. "I have two small girls who spent the day with my sister and her family. They love their aunt and uncle."

"Why didn't you join them?"

Ruby shrugged. "I don't know. I thought it would be nice for them to see the fireworks and be away from their overprotective mum for a change, I suppose. Whose side are you on, anyway?"

Brett clasped his hands on the table. "I'm just alerting you to the kinds of questions you are likely to be receiving when you are on the witness stand. You all need to be sure of your answers. Let's call it a day and reconvene here tomorrow afternoon, same time." He escorted the ladies to the elevator.

Goldie turned. "You didn't even ask if I was actually guilty."

The attorney stared back at her and her friends. There was something about them that he couldn't help but warm to. "You all claim to have the iron-clad alibi. I must take you at your word."

*****

Brett looked at his watch. *Well at least they're punctual,* he thought when he heard the ladies chatting as they entered the lobby the next day. He greeted them at the doorway. "Come this way, ladies," he said, beckoning them into his office. "Can I pour you some coffee?"

They all sat down.

Ruby placed her purse on the floor. "Is that the best you have to offer?" she asked jokingly.

Brett laughed. "Well, my secretary made me a fresh pot. I sure wouldn't want it to go to waste." He poured himself a cup. They all declined.

"I can't stand the suspense. What does the DA claim to have against me?" asked Goldie.

Very carefully worded, observed the lawyer. "Remember, it is not the DA, it is Madge Williams who works for the DA's office who is handling the case. It seems they have Detective Cooper and his assistant, Len Tyler, and a gentleman by the name of Gordon Roscoe."

Before he could go any further, Goldie interrupted him. "Who the hell is he? I don't know any Gordon, let alone a Gordon Roscoe." She looked at Satin and Ruby for help. Both shook their heads.

"Well, whoever he is. He has some information. I guess we'll have to wait for the trial to find out," Brett said. "They also have a Mrs. Wendy Moorlands, a Ms. Claudia O'Shaughnessy, and a Dr. Thelma Priestly."

"What?" cried Goldie in a state of genuine shock. "Wendy Moorlands ran the rehab center I was at recently. I shared a room with Claudia, and Dr. Priestly was the onsite therapist. What in the world have they got to do with anything? And I thought Claudia was a friend. That bitch."

Brett took a gulp of his coffee. "You might want to keep those types of sentiments to yourself, if and when you are on the stand. What is more troubling to me is they have on their list the neighbors, Mr. and Mrs. Godfrey."

Satin was astounded. "Impossible! There is no way the Kravitzes could deny us all being at my home."

"I would agree," said Ruby. "It's just not possible."

Brett leaned forward onto his desk. "They could be hostile witnesses for all I know. Naturally, the case is at its preliminary stages. Madge is still miffed over being caught short yesterday. But I've worked with her before. She'll simmer down over time."

"From the way you said that, does that mean ... do we have a deal?" asked Satin.

"That depends. I'd like to ask if there is anything else I should know?" Brett was sure they were concealing information from him. "Anything else I should be aware of? Like Goldie here being in a rehab center — by the way, why were you in there?"

Goldie was never one to pull her punches, and she wasn't going to start now. "I was a drug addict. I didn't think it was relevant to the case though. And I've been clean since I was released."

"Congratulations!" The lawyer was sincere in his response.

"Come on now, Brett. Do we have a deal or what?" Satin asked for a second time.

He was torn. The attorney looked down at his desk and twiddled his thumbs. He was in a real predicament. *There's really no reward here,* he thought. *I either run the risk of ruining my career, or I run the risk of ruining my family and, possibly, my life. I know it is pointless for me to ask them if they want to plea bargain.* "Yes," he said, hesitating briefly. "We have a deal."

Ruby tried to lighten the solemnity. "Well, you don't have to sound so somber about it. I think this calls for a celebration. Now, you must have some champagne here." She rose from her seat, strolled to the wet bar, and opened the wine refrigerator. "Aha," she exclaimed, pulling a bottle of champagne from the cooler. "Perrier Jouet. Not exactly Dom Perignon, but it'll do." She popped the cork and poured four glasses. Ruby raised her glass. "Here's to justice."

Goldie stopped her. "To hell with justice. Here's to my freedom."

"Wait a minute," Brett said. "What guarantee do I have that you will keep your end of the bargain?"

Satin raised her glass and winked at him. "Mr. Perry Mason. The name of our company is Discreetly Yours. We practice what we preach. Our word is our bond. You can trust us completely. Here's to a great working relationship."

He smiled, albeit nervously, yet for some reason, he believed them.

The four of them clinked their glasses.

"To freedom!" they said in unison.

CHAPTER 25

T hanksgiving and Christmas rolled around. It was a somber holiday season for Ruby, Satin, and particularly, Goldie. It was a relief for them to finally receive news on New Year's Eve that the trial was set for the end of January. They decided to ring in the New Year with a celebration by hosting a catered party at the office for all the escorts. Everyone was there except for Ruby, who stayed home with her daughters.

"Sorry I couldn't be there," Ruby said to Satin through the phone. "It's been so quiet here. The girls and I watched the ball drop from Times Square on TV. I just put them to bed, bless their hearts, and I wanted to call and wish you all a Happy New Year. How is it going?"

"It was a small turnout," said Satin. "But that's because most of the escorts had dates. Good for our business. As you well know, New Years is always one of the busiest nights of the year."

"And the last ones here got late calls," added Goldie. "They left around eleven o'clock. You know, the usual last-minute calls, clients seeking someone to keep them company. I guess no one wants to spend New Year's Eve alone."

"Well, I'm glad we're out of the game — I'm not sure if I could stay awake long enough for a date tonight. I'm ready to hit the sack. How did the girls who came like the bonuses?"

"They were thrilled. Never had anything like that from Frankie. They're all very happy with the split since we took over the company. Both the men and the women. Even with the bail money, we're still in good shape."

They wished each other a Happy New Year and hung up. The two women started to tidy up. Satin wrapped the remaining food in bags and filled the refrigerator. Goldie collected the dirty paper plates and plastic cups that were scattered throughout the office and deposited them in a trash bag. "How could so few people make such a mess?" she asked. Finally, when the cleanup work was done, the girls sat down to relax.

"It seems strange not to be working tonight, doesn't it?" Goldie asked, popping a champagne cork and pouring both of them another glass. "I have to wonder what Harvey is doing this evening."

They toasted each other as they kicked back, both putting their feet up on the desk. They could hear the fireworks shooting off on the Strip and heard the throngs of people making merry on the street below. The honking of car horns never seemed to stop.

"Who's Harvey?" asked Satin.

"He's that weirdo I met at that charity function, remember?"

"Oh yes, that's right." Satin yawned. "My God, I'm exhausted!" She threw her head back and ran her fingers through her hair. "Yes, it does seem strange not to be out there. But I must confess — I don't miss it, and I am happy being partners with the two of you. We've done really well."

"I don't miss it either. I'm enjoying the partnership too. Just hope the New Year promises to be a good one."

Satin stretched out her hand and patted Goldie on the wrist. "Don't worry, it will. You'll get off scot-free." She didn't want Goldie to get depressed by dwelling on the subject, so she switched gears. "And look how well you're doing without the drugs. You're really turning your life around."

"Yeah, it's tough, though. I won't deny it. Thank God for you and Ruby. Both of you have really been like the Rock of Gibraltar for me." She smiled and grabbed Satin's hand. "Thank you."

Satin returned the smile. "Well, I guess it's time to pack up and go home, huh?"

Goldie gathered her purse from the floor and rose from the chair. "At least it was good news to hear about the trial date."

Satin's cellphone rang. Recognizing Richard's phone number, she gave Goldie a big hug. "I need to take this call. Happy New Year, Goldie. We'll chat soon. Help yourself to whatever's in the refrigerator."

They hugged, and she watched Goldie leave the room.

"Well hello, Richard. To what do I owe this honor?" She peered through the window at the busy spectacle outside.

Richard was slightly nervous, wondering if she was with someone. "Are you alone?"

"Of course I'm alone," she responded. "We've just wrapped up our company New Year's Eve party. Happy New Year to you, by the way."

"I just got home from a party. Happy New Year to you, too."

"It will be happy if you have good news about my friend's court case."

Richard sighed. "I told you, I can't get involved. I must stay out of it."

Satin remained calm. "On the contrary, Richard. You *must* get involved. I need you to be the judge."

"No, Satin. When you called me and asked if I would preside over your friend's bail case, I told you at the time I could not be part of your plan."

"And I told you I needed your help. You did it then, and you can do it now," Satin retorted.

"I will not get embroiled in this case, and that's final. If you say anything publicly about our relationship, it will be your word against mine. And the public will be more likely to believe a well-respected judge."

Now Satin was annoyed. "Don't play heavy-handed with me, Richard. They will not believe you. I have hardcore evidence to prove it. I will not hesitate to use it, if needed."

"That's blackmail." He wondered whether she had video or audio tapes of their tryst. How was he to know she had the books and the money with his fingerprints locked in her safe?

"No, it's called being a friend. That prosecutor from the DA's office is on a miserable fishing expedition. You *will* find a way to be the presiding judge, Richard."

He was taken aback by her assertive manner, but sensed she was not bluffing. "I'm almost sorry I called. I just wanted to wish you the best for the New Year."

"I wish you the same, too, Richard — not to mention your wife and daughter, Deidre. It will be a good year if you get yourself on board with this case."

Chastened, Richard hung up.

A thought suddenly came to Satin's mind. She opened the laptop and typed away at the keyboard. She was astounded when she saw the results of her search displayed on the screen.

Well, well, well. This is a surprise. What a stroke of good fortune. I think I've just discovered our ace in the hole.

CHAPTER 26

"All rise," announced the bailiff. "The Honorable Judge Richard Cavishaw presiding." The judge entered to the muffled sounds of the public and the jury stirring in their seats. "This is the case of the State of Nevada v. Berelowitz," continued the stern-looking bailiff. "You may be seated."

Goldie was nervous and fidgeted with the buttons on her blue jacket as she tried to assess the judge by studying his face. She listened to his guidance and instructions to the jury. As his voice droned on, her concentration drifted, and she turned her eyes to all the jurors who seemed mesmerized by his preaching. *What a grab-bag of individuals. And to think this group will be deciding my fate.* It was true. There certainly was a cross-section of the community — men and women, all ages, all races. She observed a couple of ladies dressed in very smart apparel, while another bared her midriff. Two men sat next to each other at the end of the row- an impeccably dressed African-american; the other, unshaven and sporting faded jeans that were ripped and frayed. *I've seen homeless people who look better than him,* thought Goldie. *How I wish Ruby and Satin could be here with me. It's stupid that they can't be in the courtroom just because they're witnesses. Who makes up these dumb rules anyway?*

Her mind snapped back into focus when she saw the prosecutor, Madge Williams — sporting a dowdy, brown tweed skirt and matching jacket —head toward the jury to make her opening statement. Goldie listened in disbelief as to how the prosecution had evidence to prove beyond a reasonable doubt that she was guilty of murdering Frankie. She continued fiddling with the buttons on her jacket, casting her eyes downward. *I pity the poor guy who married her. Her voice is so shrill and irritating. I can't imagine listening to that before going to sleep every night. Gosh, come to think of it, perish the thought of waking up to it every morning.*

Brett was scribbling a few notes as she laid out her case. He had seen her in action before and knew her playbook. This case was no different.

"The first witness I intend to call to the stand will be the detective who worked so tirelessly on this case," Madge asserted. Pacing back and forth in front of the jury, she continued to identify the witnesses who would be presented after Detective Cooper, stressing how their testimonies would all point toward Goldie's guilt. He was to be followed by the Godfrey's and Gordon Roscoe, a homeless man who was in the vicinity on the day of the murder. The remaining three witnesses were the staff and Goldie's roommate from the rehab center.

"By the end of this trial, there will be no doubt that the murder of the crime upon which you will be asked to render a verdict, was committed by the lady seated next to the defense attorney, Ms. Gloriana Berelowitz." Madge Williams pointed her finger at Goldie and paused for effect. Her opening completed, she returned to her seat.

Brett leaped out of his chair with such fervor, Goldie jumped. "Ladies and gentlemen of the jury," he said with a forceful tone — one Goldie had not detected in their conversations. "The prosecution will attempt to persuade you with all kinds of smoke and mirror tactics, but you are required and bound by law to make your decision based on cold hard facts. In this case, there are none." Clutching the railing in front of the jury, he continued, "The police do not have the murder weapon, and they cannot place the accused at the scene of the crime. The defense will provide ample proof from witnesses that my client has a cast-iron alibi at the time the murder was purportedly committed. You will have no option but to deliver a verdict of not guilty." He looked at the faces of each one of the jurors before returning to his seat.

Masterful, thought Goldie. *Short, sweet, and to the point.* For the first time, she felt totally comfortable with her legal counsel.

"The prosecution may call its first witness," Judge Cavishaw said from behind the bench.

"The prosecution calls Detective William Cooper to the stand."

Detective Cooper swaggered into the courtroom, hands in the pockets of his overcoat. The bailiff swore him in, while Goldie chuckled softly under her breath. *Would have thought he could have left his Columbo coat outside the door. Satin and Ruby would have gotten a kick out of this.*

After providing a litany of Cooper's credentials, the prosecutor finally got to the heart of the questions. For all his expertise, Goldie was surprised at his relatively weak answers. He provided much information on the timeframe of the murder, and pointed out that the neighbors only observed the three ladies on the patio for certain periods of time. He flicked through his notepad, referring to this time and that, explaining how it was plausible that sufficient time could have lapsed for two of the ladies to drive to the scene of the crime and return in plenty of time to be seen by the neighbors. The detective testified that the homeless man had been interviewed and confirmed he had seen a lady fitting Goldie's description. He saw her leave the building where the murder took place at the same time the murder occurred.

Brett could not wait for his turn to cross-examine the witness. Leaving his desk, he started to parade around the area in front of the witness box, occasionally facing the jury for impact. "So, Detective Cooper, do you have the murder weapon?"

"No."

"Did you find any fingerprints on the body? Or any DNA?"

"Negative."

"Was my client found anywhere near the victim at the time of his death?"

"No, but she was in the vicinity. She was seen leaving the building where the murder took place."

"Ah, yes. According to a homeless man, right?" His voice dripped with sarcasm. "I can't wait to hear his testimony later."

"Objection!" Madge yelled from her desk.

"Sustained," ordered the judge. "You know better than that, Mr. Lamont."

"My apologies, Your Honor," Brett acknowledged perfunctorily. "And how did my client leave the building? Did she take a bus or hail a cab?"

"No, she departed in a waiting car, which I believe belonged to her accomplice, Rhonda Smallwell."

Goldie was taken aback. *Wow. I wonder how he was able to link Ruby to the crime.*

"Oh? If you believe she was an accomplice, why didn't you arrest Ms. Smallwell as a co-conspirator?" Brett asked.

The detective looked down. "We cannot be sure."

"Why is that? Surely your witness was able to identify the vehicle?"

"No, not with any degree of certainty."

"What? Not even the license plate number?"

"Negative," Cooper said quietly.

"Could you please speak up, Detective Cooper, so the jury can hear?"

"I said 'negative.'"

"Detective, my witnesses will attest that Ms. Smallwell and my client carpooled to the barbecue in my client's car. The car remained parked outside the house until the barbecue was over — hours after the murder took place. How do you account for that?"

"I can't, Mr. Lamont. Perhaps there was a car in the back alley or on a side street."

"Have you been able to find any such vehicle?"

"No, I haven't."

"Do you have an exact time of the victim's death?"

"Not exactly."

Brett turned away from the witness and faced the jury.

"Simply put, Detective Cooper, I would say your testimony is entirely circumstantial and hypothetical, wouldn't you? There's no weapon. Sure, there's one witness who claims he may have seen a woman fitting my client's description somewhere in the area, yet there's no evidence that she left the party. And most importantly, there's no motive."

"Let's assume there was a car waiting on a side street," he continued, one hand on his hip, the other gesticulating wildly. "For my client to get from the barbecue to the victim's office, commit the crime, and return to the barbecue, it would require split-second timing. It would have to have occurred at the precise time of the victim's death, which you can't even identify." He threw his hands in the air.

Wow, I really am liking this guy, thought Goldie, clapping her hands together quietly beneath the table.

Detective Cooper was irritated. "We have an approximate time of the victim's death. And my hunches tell me your client committed the crime, Sir. In all the years I have been with the force, I've never been wrong about a hunch."

"Your Honor, I request that the last remark be stricken from the record, and for the jury to be instructed to ignore it."

Madge rose to her feet again. "Objection, Your Honor. The witness is certainly entitled to call on his years of experience."

"It's prejudicial, Your Honor. The district attorney's office knows that."

The judge banged the gavel. "Objection sustained. The jury is to disregard the last statement from the witness."

"Thank you, Your Honor. Fortunately for my client, our system of justice requires guilt to be proven beyond a reasonable doubt. Unfortunately for you, Detective Cooper, hunches don't hold up in court."

"Objection!" Madge hollered.

The judge banged the gavel again. "Mr. Lamont, I will have no grandstanding in my courtroom. Do I make myself clear?"

"My apologies, Your Honor. I have no further questions for this *expert* witness."

Detecting the sarcasm in his voice, Madge objected again.

"The witness is excused," Judge Cavishaw said. "As for you, Mr. Lamont, I will not warn you again. This court will stand in recess for lunch until two o'clock. I expect you will reevaluate your conduct in this courtroom. I do not wish to jeopardize your client with contempt of court charges."

Goldie was relieved for a break. The tension in room was making her anxious. *Good grief, this judge sure runs a tight ship, and the trial has hardly started.*

CHAPTER 27

Brett and Goldie walked out of the courthouse together. It had been a long day. She extended her hand. "Thank you, counselor. I was very impressed with your performance in the courtroom today — first, with Columbo this morning and then the neighbors this afternoon. I just know you're going to win this case for me."

Brett was clutching his briefcase with one hand and courteously accepted her handshake with the other. "Don't be too sure." He started toward the parking lot.

"But you totally demolished the testimony of both Detective Cooper and the neighbors. I don't understand why the prosecution would have wanted them to testify."

Brett stopped and turned to face his client. "Both the Godfrey's testified to the fact that there was an extended period of time when you were out of their sight."

"But they couldn't specify for how long or when," Goldie said. "You raised the doubt."

"We don't know that. It's up to the jury to make that determination. Remember, we're still in the early stages. We don't know what Madge still has up her sleeve. As a recovering drug addict, you of all people should know to take it one day at a time. In the meantime, I'll remind you that you are not permitted to see or engage in conversation with any of the upcoming witnesses. I know how close you are with your cohorts and probably already arranged a meeting with them somewhere this evening. Just don't tell me or anyone else about it. I hope you grasp the gravity of what I am telling you."

"Understood, counselor. Thank you. See you tomorrow at 9:30 sharp."

She climbed into her car and drove out of the parking lot. *Well, he's right about one thing, I do have a meeting with Satin and Ruby.* The three women agreed to meet every day after court, so all would be kept abreast of what transpired.

Brett started his drive home, too. One side of his brain went into automatic steering mode as he turned onto the freeway, while the other side went into overdrive. *In all the years I've been practicing law, I've never had a case or a client like this one. It's just as well that I don't know for sure whether she is innocent or guilty. She is right though — I'm not sure what advantage there was for the prosecution bringing the neighbors to the stand.* He shook his head. *True, they did state there was a period of time when Gloriana was not in sight, but at least they established her presence at the barbecue. Can't imagine what Madge was thinking. I thought she had more evidence than what was presented. Probably would have been better letting me call them as witnesses, then casting doubt on the alibi by highlighting the timeframe when Gloriana was not visible. Foolish of her to establish the alibi and allow me to cast doubt. Defense one, prosecution zero.* He smiled, and his car automatically turned onto the beltway, as if it knew its own way home. *And then there was Detective Cooper. He got so bogged down in the time schedule, it must have bored the hell out of the jury — or at least confused the hell out of them. Not bad for our first day, if I say so myself. But still waiting for the bombshell ... if Madge has one.*

Steering her car in the opposite direction, Goldie looked in her rearview mirror and made a couple of diversionary turns onto side roads to make sure she was not being followed — a precautionary measure the three had agreed upon while the trial was in progress. Upon satisfying herself that no car was trailing her, she finally headed to the Desert Bar and Grill. It was the same restaurant she had enjoyed her meal after she was released on bail. *I'm ready for another big, fat, juicy steak with a giant-sized baked potato.* She was in a celebratory mood. As she arrived at her destination, Goldie saw Satin and Ruby's cars in the parking lot. Her hand fumbled under the driver's seat for the bag containing her wig. Making sure nobody was in sight, she quickly placed it on her head adjusting it in the mirror. She didn't see her two friends when she first walked into the dimly lit restaurant, but she finally spotted them huddled in a small booth in the corner.

"You both look fantastic," she gushed. "Where did you get your new wigs?"

Satin gave her friend a hug. "Never mind that, don't keep us in suspense. How did it go in court today?"

Goldie went to the other side of the booth and embraced Ruby, who was seated in the middle.

"Satin's right. Like the *National Enquirer* says, enquiring minds want to know," Ruby said, though she could tell from the expression on Goldie's face that it must have went well.

"I've got to tell you, Brett Lamont was masterful. Madge Williams, the prosecutor, is a battle-axe. Her opening statement was so dramatic, and she had Columbo as her first witness. Brett demolished his testimony on the cross-examination. He then made Gladys and Abner Kravitz look like idiots. I'm thrilled with our own personal Perry Mason. I've got a feeling he's going to get me off. Thanks for finding him, Satin." She stretched her hand across the table and reached for Satin's.

Satin grinned. "Forget about Brett. Who's the judge assigned to the trial?"

"Someone called Judge Richard Cavisham or Cavishaw. Something like that."

So he managed to get himself on this trial. Well, bless his heart. I guess I owe him one. Satin was pleased at this turn of events, but she decided not to let on to her friends about her tryst just yet.

Ruby was perplexed. "Who gives a damn about the judge? It's the jury she needs to worry about. What did Brett do to discredit Detective Cooper? Is Brett done with him?"

Goldie described the events of the day in vivid detail, stopping only when their food and champagne arrived.

"Columbo and the Kravitzes were the only witnesses on the stand today. After both opening statements were made, Madge questioned Detective Cooper and allowed him to babble on about this time and that time. Even *my* eyes glazed over. But Brett was able to question the timeframe. He drove his points home and, hopefully, cast sufficient doubt in the mind of the jury. And as for the Kravitzes, they're not too sharp, are they?"

"They're probably not the brightest bulbs on the tree," Satin said. "It does sound like Brett did a pretty good job, though. Maybe we all underestimated him."

"So, do you know who the witnesses are tomorrow?" asked Ruby.

Goldie was devouring her steak. "Yes," she said, between bites. "The first witness is Gordon Roscoe. Apparently, he's some homeless guy who saw me at the building."

"Wow! I wonder if he was the same guy I gave fifty-dollars, while I was waiting for you that day, Goldie."

"What?" Satin was aghast. "You mean you saw and spoke to someone while you were outside Frankie's building and never told us? That could throw a monkey wrench into the whole scheme."

Ruby shrugged. "You knew. We discussed it when Goldie and I returned from our mission. The man was homeless. Doubt if he knew what day of the week it was, much less the time of day. Besides, I was so preoccupied with Goldie and our plan, I didn't think anything of it. I didn't even realize I gave him a fifty-dollar bill until I got home that night."

"That's right. I remember now," said Satin, somewhat disappointed he was now a witness.

Goldie sensed Satin was discouraged and tried to calm her. "Don't worry, Satin. Even if it is the same guy — apparently, he can't identify the car and didn't even get the license plate number, according to Columbo."

Ruby was still a little concerned over the possible coincidence that it could be the same person she'd helped. "How in the world did they even find him? Cooper's sidekick probably spent days interviewing street people. Our tax dollars at work."

"Well, they're all done with Cooper and the Kravitzes, and I'm not sure that any of them really helped the prosecution at all."

Ruby looked at her watch. "I need to get home to my girls. Where are we meeting tomorrow night? How about Don Quixote's? It's small and off the beaten path."

They agreed, paid their bill in cash, and embraced each other as they headed toward their cars.

Once inside her Jaguar convertible, Satin lit a cigarette and called Richard.

"What in the blazes are you doing calling me?" he answered angrily. "We can get into serious trouble having any kind of conversation."

Satin ignored his tone. "I just wanted to thank you. I'm 100 percent confident you'll give her a fair hearing."

"How do you know what case I am hearing? Were you at the court today? Have you been talking to any of the jurors?"

"Now, Judge Cavishaw." Satin was in a teasing mood. Everything was going her way. She had the attorney and the judge under her thumb. Plus, she still had her ace in the hole secret. "You know better than to ask me questions like that. You surely don't want to hear the answer, do you?"

"You know I could be thrown off the bench for having this discussion." He hung up.

"And we wouldn't want that to happen now, would we Judge Cavishaw?" she said aloud. Satin extinguished her cigarette, started her car, and headed home.

CHAPTER 28

The jurors were all in their assigned seats, and the bailiff called the court to order for the second day of the trial. Madge Williams rose from her chair and called Gordon Roscoe to the stand.

Goldie eyed her nemesis up and down. *Jeez, same boring outfit she wore yesterday, only in blue. Guess the battle-axe sees something she likes and buys it in every color. Her life is probably just as humdrum.* As the witness headed to the stand, Goldie whispered to her attorney, "I've never seen this person in my life." She focused her attention on the man who had his hand raised to swear in. *For a homeless guy, he sure looks pretty dapper with his wavy gray hair and neatly trimmed mustache, even if his face is a little scraggly. But if he's homeless, how can he afford such smart clothes?*

As Madge droned on with her examination, Goldie wondered whether she would ever get to the point. She cast her eyes to the jury to see if they were paying attention. There was an endless string of questions as to what the witness was doing outside the building, how long he'd been there that day, how could he be sure of the day, whether he was a drug addict or an alcoholic. Even Brett was beginning to wonder where all the questions were leading. He was about to ask for relevance when, without warning, the Madge pulled a wig from her briefcase.

"Your Honor, it appears the defendant was wearing a wig on the day in question in an attempt to disguise herself. I would ask that she wear this wig in order for the witness to identify her."

Brett leaped out of his seat. "Objection, Your Honor. The prosecution is obviously going to ask the witness to see if he recognizes the person in the courtroom as the one who he saw on the day in question. By asking the defendant to wear a wig directs the witness to focus on my client. This is highly suggestive and prejudicial."

"Objection sustained," said the judge.

"But, Your Honor," protested the prosecutor. "How else can my witness properly identify the accused if he is not permitted to see an accurate portrayal of the individual he claims to have seen? Nevada law permits it."

"Move on, Ms. Williams. I'm not buying it. You'll have to find another way. Such antics will not be permitted in my courtroom. Continue down another road."

The prosecutor pulled a sheet of paper from her briefcase and strode over to the witness box. "Mr. Roscoe, is this the picture the police sketch artist drew based on your description of the suspect?"

"Well, it might be, but I can't say for certain," he replied.

Madge was taken aback. "What do you mean? Doesn't this reflect the individual you saw leaving the building on the day in question?"

"As I stated, I'm not sure. The person I recall seeing was a little rounder in the face and had longer hair. I'm not sure about any of her features, like her eyes and mouth, as she was too far away. I only had a quick glance, you know. It wasn't like I was paying any particular attention."

"But this picture was drawn from your description, correct?"

The witness shrugged. "It's possible, but I can't guarantee it."

Seeing she was getting nowhere, the Madge switched gears. "You told Detective Cooper you saw the person climb into a waiting car. Could you describe the car?"

"No."

"But I thought you originally told the detective it was a red Audi."

"I said it might have been an Audi, but I couldn't be certain. I also couldn't be certain of the color. I told you, I really wasn't paying any attention. I was just minding my own business."

"May I remind you, Mr. Roscoe, you are under oath?"

"I'm aware of that, Ma'am. I'm answering as best I can."

She shook her head and momentarily pondered whether or not to ask permission to treat Mr. Roscoe as a hostile witness, but thought better of it. Seemingly irritated, she returned to her seat. "I have no further questions for this witness."

It was Brett's turn to cross-examine. "Mr. Roscoe, were you able to obtain the license plate of the car?" Having seen how the witness had contradicted the previously obtained testimony of the color and make of the car, he was sure the witness would have no knowledge of the license plate number. He wanted to drive this point home.

"No, Sir. It was not close enough, and like I said, I was not paying that much attention. You know what I mean? Besides, I think I'd downed a few beers that day, which could have blurred my vision. Maybe made my memory a bit fuzzy, too." He chuckled at his own joke.

"Returning to the sketch for a minute, since the composite presented doesn't quite fit your recollection of what you described to the sketch artist, are you suggesting the department drew another sketch to fit their own narrative?"

"I'm not sure, Sir. It all happened quite a while ago. And it's possible I didn't do a good job of describing the lady I saw."

"Did Detective Cooper prompt you as you were working with the sketch artist?"

"Well, Detective Cooper wasn't there with me. It was his assistant. I think his name was Mr. Tyler. He kept asking me questions like, 'Wasn't her face thinner?' and 'Wasn't her hair shorter?'"

"Sounds like he was leading you, Mr. Roscoe?"

"Objection," Madge shouted.

Now it was the judges turn to be irritated. "Sustained! The jury will disregard the comment from the defense attorney. Your last warning, Mr. Lamont."

"I apologize, Your Honor. I have no more questions for this witness."

"You may step down," the judge advised. "The court will stand in recess until two o' clock."

Madge stormed out of the courtroom and called Detective Cooper. "I'm absolutely furious," she said. "We had Roscoe on the stand this morning. He may have been pretty sure of himself to you, but he sure was as vague as hell on the witness stand. I felt like a real idiot."

Detective Cooper was in his office, when the call came in. He removed his feet from the desk, and sat bolt upright. "Why? What happened?"

"First, Judge Cavishaw wouldn't allow me to use the wig. Then, Roscoe backed off the sketch and finally claimed he was unsure about the color and make of the car."

"Someone must have gotten to him. He was pretty sure of himself when we interviewed him."

"Oh, you haven't heard the best of it yet, Cooper. Roscoe now says he'd downed a few drinks that day, so his vision may have been blurry and his memory could have been fuzzy. Why didn't you ask him if he'd been drinking?"

"Hey, don't get mad at me, Madge. You interviewed him, too. You could have asked him if he'd been drinking."

She backed off. "You're right. I'm sorry. I just didn't think he'd back away from everything like he did."

"Who do you have coming up?"

"This afternoon will be the setup witnesses — the roomie the defendant had at the rehab center, as well as the director. Things should go smoothly, provided no one has gotten to them, too. I'm saving the big gun for tomorrow."

*****

Goldie followed Brett down the steps of the courthouse. She was not as happy with him as she was the day before. "Hey, counselor, what did you mean by letting those two bitches off so lightly this afternoon? They crucified me on the stand, and you let them get away with it."

Brett turned to look at her. "Will you back off and just let me do what you are not paying me to do? There was nothing to be gained from cross-examining those witnesses. Your roommate at the rehab center said you talked in your sleep once or twice about murdering someone."

"But she vilified me. All those hateful things she said."

"All the more reason not to cross-examine. Even the prosecution had to ask her to restrict her answers to the questions asked. The animus potentially created some sympathy for you. As for you talking in your sleep ... well, we all have dreams and nightmares. Doesn't mean they're based on facts. It doesn't take a rocket scientist to figure that out. Any reasonable-minded person can deduce that. The director, Wendy Moorlands, basically made that case while she was on the stand. When Claudia discussed your sleep talking with Wendy, even she had to check with the therapist to find out how to handle it. Incidentally, Dr. Thelma Priestly will be taking the stand tomorrow. How was your relationship with her?"

Goldie shrugged. "About the same as those two old broads who testified this afternoon. I really didn't get along with any of them. I kept to myself as much as possible."

"We'll see what the doctor has to say tomorrow. The two ladies this afternoon didn't do you too much damage, and Mr. Roscoe almost helped you. You go home now, and get a good night's sleep. Let me go and do my preparation."

He turned and headed toward his car. Goldie watched him leave before she crossed the street to the parking structure. She climbed the stairs and fumbled in her purse for the car keys. She was glad the area was well-lit, but the sound of footsteps heading in her direction made her nervous. The lot was otherwise eerily quiet. Instinctively, she turned around and was stunned to see who was standing in front of her. She dropped her purse. "Mr. Roscoe. You scared me. Why are you following me?"

He smiled at her. "Ma'am, we need to talk."

CHAPTER 29

"**Y**ou know we shouldn't be talking like this," whispered Goldie, trying not to sound too frightened. "You could get us both into trouble." She took a good look at Gordon Roscoe — the lines on his face reflected a tough and fully lived life.

"I know, Ma'am. I promise I won't keep you for long. Why don't you open your car door, and I'll sit on the floor against the wall on the other side? That way, no one can see me. And if someone does come, I'll be able to hear them, and I'll shut up. You just keep fumbling for your keys." He picked up her purse and handed it to her.

Goldie was at a loss. Despite her fear, her curiosity got the better of her, and she opened the door. He immediately crouched behind it and leaned back against the wall.

"I deliberately misled the prosecution in your case today. I'm not stupid. I knew the make of the car. I recognized you and could have identified you with or without the wig. I hadn't even had anything to drink that day. My eyes weren't blurry in the slightest. I could see as clear as a bell. At first, when I was interviewed by the police, I wasn't aware they were tracking you down for murder. I only found out about that later."

Goldie was confused. "I don't understand."

"I don't know whether you killed anyone or not. I don't even care." He shrugged. "I do know the lady whose car you got into that day. She is one classy dame." He shook his head as he recalled the events of the Fourth of July. "I was a homeless veteran. She gave me fifty bucks. I hadn't seen that much money for ages."

Goldie didn't have the heart to tell him that Ruby wasn't aware it was a fifty-dollar bill when she gave it to him.

"After she gave me that money, I went across the road to the coffee shop. The owner knows me and often gives me day-old donuts if I go to the back door. This time, I went in and ordered a pot roast. It was piping hot, served on a china plate with a warm, fresh bread roll. It was amazing. It made me feel like a human being again. I had the money to catch a bus to one of the missions, where I prayed. I actually cried."

He paused as he wiped his forehead. "A minister came and sat next to me. We chatted for a while. I was ready to turn my life around. It was like divine intervention. He found me a halfway house and even fixed me up with a job. Yeah, it's just menial work mowing lawns and weeding gardens at some of his friend's homes. But I've been doing it ever since. Pay isn't great, but I have a small studio apartment now. Nothing much in it, just a mattress on the floor and a few other things. A couple pieces of clothing to hang in a tiny closet. But it's a start."

He looked into Goldie's eyes. "My entire life changed because of the goodness of your friend's heart. I saw you climb into her car. And I don't believe that she could ever be involved in a murder." He paused.

If only this guy knew how Ruby was up to her eyeballs in this murder, thought Goldie, as she listened to his outpouring and realized what a lucky break this was.

"I've been waiting outside the courthouse since I was dismissed today. I just want you to thank your friend for me, God bless her. I wanted to write a little card or something, but my writing's bad and my hand's a little shaky."

They both heard a car start from the parking level above. Goldie quickly opened the rear door of the car and acted as though she was putting something on the back seat. She waited until the car screeched past her and disappeared to the floor below before closing the door. True to his word, Gordon kept quiet, not that anyone would have heard, given the sound of the tires as they spun rapidly around the corners.

Goldie offered him a cigarette, which he declined. "I'll be sure to pass on your message — and thank you. But before you go, I have one question. How did the police even know where to find you?"

"Oh, that. Well, as I said, I used to go to the coffee shop across the street. All the managers knew me. I'd been there earlier that day, and they gave me some water and a blueberry muffin. It was a fresh muffin. Guess they wanted to treat me well, it being Independence Day and all. A few days later, that detective stopped by the diner and asked if any of the staff had seen anything. One of the managers said I was at the coffee shop that day and might have seen something. Of course, I wasn't there at the time the detective questioned the folks in the coffee shop, but they were all told to call him next time I stopped by. It was a couple of days later when I went to see if there were any day-old donuts, and that's when the detective was called. Boy, he sure got there fast. I hadn't even finished licking the sugar from the donut off of my fingers, and there he was … asking questions."

The door to the stairwell opened, and a couple headed toward their car, chatting and laughing as they went. Goldie busied herself in the backseat again. She heard their car doors slam. The engine started, and she waited for the sound to fade as it made its way toward the exit.

"Look, I can't thank you enough for what you have done, and for your thoughts about my friend. You're absolutely right about her. She has a heart of gold. I'll let her know how you're doing. I'm sure she will be thrilled to hear about your life-changing experience." She opened her purse, pulled out a couple of twenty-dollar bills, and handed them to him. He stood up.

"Here, take these and treat yourself to a nice dinner," she continued. "I don't mean to be rude, but I must go. If we're caught, we're both dead." She felt awkward and didn't want to seem ungrateful. "I'd hate anything to happen to you," she added. "You know, after you've made such a terrific turnaround in your life."

"You're right, Ma'am. I just want you to thank your friend for me. You don't need to give me this money." He tried to return the bills.

She closed her hand over his. "I insist. You keep it."

"Well, God bless you, Ma'am. And good luck with your trial."

Before she knew it, he disappeared through the doorway, and she heard his footsteps as he went downstairs.

Before leaving the parking structure, she donned her wig. *Thank God, the lights are bright here. Easier than trying to put it on in the restaurant parking lot.* After doing the customary detours, she finally arrived to Don Quixote's to meet Satin and Ruby.

Once again, she was the last to arrive.

"So, how did it go today?" were the first words out of Satin's mouth. "By the way, we ordered you a strawberry margarita. We know how much you like those when we come here."

Goldie was bubbling with enthusiasm. "You won't believe what happened."

She proceeded to recap her meeting with Gordon Roscoe and the testimony of the two witnesses from the rehab center.

"All sounds fantastic. Ruby and I have more good news for you, my friend. Our escorts all chipped in and collected nearly three thousand dollars to help cover the cost of your defense."

The tears started to roll down Goldie's face. "Are you serious? I never knew they cared so much."

Satin nodded. "Incredible isn't it? We're blessed to have such a good bunch. La crème de la crème as Miss Jean

Brodie would say. Of course, they don't know we're getting your defense pro bono."

"I'm speechless," said Ruby, who had hung on every word Goldie was saying while dismissing Satin's comments about the collection. "Maybe that fifty-dollar bill was meant to be. Who would have thought it would have such far-reaching consequences? Maybe a guardian angel was looking down on all of us that day, after all."

The server brought their margaritas.

"Who knows? But today was a good day," said Goldie, wiping the tears away from her eyes. "And I just can't believe the crew pitched in so much money."

"Let's have a toast before we order our meal," Satin said.

They all clinked their glasses together, completely oblivious to the devastating event that was about to unfold.

CHAPTER 30

The jury trooped into the courtroom and took their assigned seats. Goldie was preoccupied watching Madge Williams stride down the aisle in yet another dreary outfit. *Her husband should give her a gift certificate for a personal shopper,* thought Goldie. *She's certainly no slave to fashion.*

The first witness called to the stand was Dr. Thelma Priestly.

"You can see why I didn't like her, can't you?" Goldie whispered to Brett. "Look at the stern expression on her face. She wears that all the time. Not exactly a warm aura about her, is there? She'd be better suited as a prison warden — she looks like a male one at that."

"Shh!" replied Brett.

He did have to agree with his client, though. The very portly, middle-aged lady with short-cropped graying hair did not strike him as a sympathetic individual. *Not exactly my idea of a hot date,* he thought, while wondering what incriminating evidence the doctor would have on his client.

After establishing her position at the rehab center, the prosecution asked for the witness' credentials. Sounding haughty and authoritative, Thelma gave a lengthy dissertation of her experience, including many degrees in psychology and psychiatry. Goldie listened intently, while the sound of Brett tapping his pencil on his yellow notepad annoyed her. She shifted back and forth in her seat, pondering what the doctor would reveal.

"Thank you, Dr. Priestly," Madge said when the witness finally finished. "While the accused was at the rehab center, did she ever confide in you that she had indeed committed a murder?"

"Yes. She explained it in detail."

"That's a lie!" Goldie shrieked, jumping up from her seat, her face flushed with anger. She shook with rage, and her hands trembled as she pounded them on the desk.

Simultaneously, Brett leapt to his feet, dropping his pencil. "Objection, Your Honor. This is an outrage."

The judge banged the gavel firmly on the table. "Mr. Lamont. Please control your client," he ordered.

Madge remained unfettered by the outburst and seized the opportunity to press her case. "And where did this confession take place, Dr. Priestly?"

"While under hypnosis," she replied. "That's why I called the police department. They connected me with Detective Cooper."

"Objection, Your Honor," Brett yelled.

Goldie pointed her finger at the witness. "You're a lying bitch!" she screamed. "I only consented to hypnosis to be cured of my drug addiction."

The courthouse erupted into chaos. The jurors started talking with each other, as did all of the attendees. Judge Cavishaw, clearly annoyed, continued banging his gavel. "Order! Order!" he shouted. "There will be order in my courtroom." His appeal fell on deaf ears. "Will one of the bailiffs please clear the court, and the other take the jurors to the jury room?" he demanded. "Counselors, I will see you both in my chambers! Now! Bailiffs, make sure there's no communication between the witness and the accused." He banged his gavel so firmly, Dr. Priestly jumped in her seat.

The public and the jury were shepherded outside, as the two attorneys followed the judge into his chambers. They had both appeared before the judge many times before and had never seen him this irate.

The judge removed his robes, threw them on the hanger, and sat firmly behind his desk. "I could have you both disbarred for this. The conduct during this trial has been highly unbecoming since the outset."

"Your Honor, I insist you declare a mistrial," Brett demanded as he slammed the door shut, while ignoring the judge's comments.

The prosecution was clearly agitated too. "You know, I'm almost inclined to agree with you. There's been something rotten about this case since day one. First, we get very short notice on the trial. Then, the bail was set ridiculously low. Where's the media? We have a murder trial, and not one article in the press about it. We've had witnesses change their testimonies, and with all due respect, Your Honor, one-sided rulings from the bench."

Now it was Judge Cavishaw's turn. He rose from his chair, rounded the desk, stood as close as he could get to Madge, and looked her straight in the eye. "I'm warning you — one more remark along those lines, and I assure you, just like that, I'll personally see to it that you are disbarred." He snapped his fingers in front of her nose to illustrate his point. "That is no idle threat, Ms. Williams. Do I make myself clear?"

She could tell from the severity in his tone that he meant every word. She secretly hoped he would not grant a mistrial, considering Dr. Priestly had clearly cast doubt in the minds of the jury as to Goldie's innocence. "Yes," she responded.

"How dare you come into my chambers and question my rulings." He then turned to Brett and imparted with equal venom, "And as for you, how dare you demand a mistrial? Your behavior here these last few days has been an embarrassment to the judicial system. There will be no mistrial. You will get back into that courtroom — both of you — and do your jobs. And you, Mr. Lamont, will instruct your client to behave herself."

"But, Your Honor," Brett implored, "the evidence provided by the witness was highly prejudicial and not permitted in a Nevada court of law. The prosecution knows information obtained from someone under hypnosis is only admissible in matters of life and death, and yet she pushed her witness knowingly."

Judge Cavishaw returned to his seat behind the desk. "The jury will be instructed to ignore the testimony of Dr. Priestly."

Clearly frustrated, Madge threw her hands in the air. "But Dr. Priestly is my key witness. She's the only one with the irrefutable evidence. I must be allowed to continue, so the details can be explained to the jury. Her testimony is compelling." She knew the judge would not permit any further presentation from the witness, but she protested, anyway. She had already scored a major triumph in getting Dr. Priestly to confirm Goldie's confession for the jury to hear.

"My ruling stands. Now both of you get back in the courtroom and do your jobs. In the meantime, I will determine what fines to impose on both of you."

The two attorneys left the chambers, while the judge put on his robes. *Madge did have a point. I wonder why there has been no media in the courtroom — nothing in the papers or on the news. My God, surely Satin can't have influence over the entire media. Could she?* He shook his head.

Back in the courtroom, the bailiffs were instructed to reconvene the jury and allow the public back inside. Once there was a semblance of order, the judge admonished the jury. "You will ignore the evidence presented by this witness. It will be stricken from the record and can have no place in your deliberations. Please continue, Ms. Williams."

"I have nothing further, Your Honor."

Brett rose from his seat. "Dr. Priestly, you don't care for my client, do you?"

"Objection. Relevance?" Madge asked.

"Goes to motive, Your Honor," the defense replied. "Even the witness must surely be aware that her testimony is not permissible in a Nevada court, since information given by an individual under hypnosis is prohibited unless otherwise stated."

Before the judge could rule, the doctor replied. "I wanted to see justice done."

Judge Cavishaw banged the gavel. "Objection overruled. Dr. Priestly, please just answer the question asked. The jury will disregard the last remark."

The doctor looked at Goldie and then at the defense attorney. The contempt oozed from her voice. "You're right. I did not like your client with her high and mighty attitude. She was disruptive, rude, arrogant, and…"

"Thank you Dr. Priestly. A simple yes or no was all I was looking for. We get the message — your obviously have a prejudice against my client. I have no more questions for this witness." Brett sat down.

The judge glanced at Dr. Priestly. "The witness is excused. The prosecution may call its next witness."

Madge rose from her seat. "The prosecution rests, Your Honor."

.

CHAPTER 31

❖

As the courtroom cleared, Brett put his pencil and notepad back in his attaché case. He looked at his client, who appeared crestfallen. "Hey, what's the cause for the gloomy look?" he asked.

"The testimony from that witch, Thelma, was pretty devastating. We're screwed, aren't we?"

"Not necessarily. The jury was instructed to ignore her comments. I finally figured out what took so long for Detective Cooper to arrest you. The neighbors and Mr. Roscoe, that was all flimsy and circumstantial evidence." He shrugged. "They could only nail you on the evidence provided by Dr. Priestly, which Cooper and Madge both know is inadmissible. I guess they just decided to go for broke. It's their only hope of convicting you."

"How do we overcome that damning testimony though?"

He smiled at her. "Well, you might try giving me a little credit for a start. It's our turn now."

"Do you know, that's the first time I've seen you smile since this whole thing started? You're kind of cute when you smile."

Brett was clearly embarrassed, and his face turned red. Goldie smiled back at him. "Don't worry. I'm not trying to make a play for you. Just making an observation. Who do you have lined up for my defense?"

"Your friends Serena Young and Rhonda Smallwell. That's all we need."

Goldie was stunned. "You mean you're not going to call me to testify?"

"No. There's nothing to be gained, and Madge would use the opportunity to unnerve you and distort anything you might say. You have two witnesses to provide the perfect alibi. In my closing statement, I'll remind the jury of the neighbor's testimony, which supported your defense just as much as damned it."

Goldie sighed. "Well, Perry Mason … you're the expert."

"I'm glad you recognize that."

He smiled again and patted her gently on the shoulder. "Now, once again, go home and get a good night's sleep. I'm going to do the same. We both have a big day tomorrow. But I assure you, the worst is over."

As Goldie drove to La Parma to meet the girls, she had a hollow feeling in her stomach. *I wish I had Brett's confidence. God, I hope I don't have to spend the rest of my life in prison.* She reached for a tissue to wipe away the tears that were rolling down her cheeks. As she pulled into the parking lot, she checked the mirror to make sure her mascara wasn't smudged. Ruby and Satin were already seated at the bar. As soon as Goldie walked in, they could tell it had not been a good day.

Goldie reached out and hugged them both. "I need a stiff drink. Do you mind if we skip the food tonight? I'm really not hungry."

"Sure. Let's go sit at the corner table over there, where we can have some peace and quiet." Satin placed her arm around Goldie.

"Works for me. Eating out every night has me a little concerned over my figure, anyway," Ruby said, hoping to lighten the tension she felt in Goldie's hug.

She turned to the bartender. "Can you please send over a double gin martini with a couple of olives for my friend?"

As soon as they were seated, Satin reached for Goldie's hand. "Are you OK? What happened? Everything was going so well yesterday."

Goldie relayed the events of the day, the pandemonium in the courthouse, and the crushing evidence presented by Dr. Priestly. Her eyes welled up with tears again, and she reached for another tissue. "That woman just hated me. I don't believe I ever said anything under hypnosis. I think she just made it up. The three of them — Priestly, Wendy, and Claudia — are thick as thieves. Yes, I might have spoken out in my sleep. I've had a few nightmares, for sure. But I can't imagine saying anything under hypnosis."

Satin grabbed a few peanuts from the bowl on the table. "I didn't know you were hypnotized when you were there. Why would they do such a thing? And what motive would she have to make up a story to hurt you?"

"I think they all thought I would have a relapse, and they didn't want me back there." Goldie blew her nose. "They must have thought that bitch's opinion would carry more weight than that of a recovering drug addict." She looked up. "God, for the first time since getting out of rehab, I'm getting a craving."

Satin and Ruby exchanged glances.

"Maybe you shouldn't be alone tonight," Satin said. "Do you want one of us to spend the night with you?"

Ruby finished her drink. "If it weren't for my two girls, you could spend the night at my house. But if Maria and Gabby overhear us talking, who knows what they might inadvertently blurt out when they're staying with my sister."

Satin nodded. "I agree. And with the Kravitzes living next door to me, not a good idea to come to my place either. I'm more than happy to spend the night at your house. We can leave my car here for the night. We'd have to come back early tomorrow, so I could go home and change for my big day on the stand."

"That's right," said Goldie. "You both have to come to court tomorrow."

"We know," replied Ruby. "The court already called us both. Don't worry. We'll give solid alibis. I'm testifying first, I've been told. I guess Lamont's saving the best for last."

Satin hit her friend playfully. "Don't be silly. But while we've been waiting for you each night, Ruby and I have been making sure we have our stories straight, without coming across as rehearsed. You know, the food we had, who brought what, the show on TV, who tossed the salad. All that stuff. We'll totally confound the battle-axe."

They all chuckled before the somber quiet. Goldie broke the silence. "Give me your honest opinion, girls. It doesn't look good for me, does it?"

"I don't know," said Satin. "The alibis are solid. I don't think the prosecution can find any way to trip us up. What does Perry Mason say about your chances?"

Goldie chuckled. "Surprisingly, he feels good about everything. He says the jury was instructed to ignore the hypnosis testimony, and that the rest of their case is weak."

Even though Satin was not convinced of the attorney's assessment, she wanted to be supportive and encouraging. "I think Lamont's right on target," she lied.

Ruby agreed, even though she had the same doubts as Satin.

Satin picked up her purse. "C'mon, let's go. I'll spend the night with you, Goldie. You'll feel better tomorrow morning, I promise."

Ruby stood up and hugged them. "Satin's right. Tomorrow will be better."

Goldie suddenly felt embarrassed. "You know, Ruby, I've been so wrapped up with myself, I haven't even asked you how Maria and Gabby are doing."

"They're getting bigger every day, and they make it all worthwhile."

"You're fortunate to have two such shining lights in your life, my friend. I just hope I'll be out of prison in time to attend their graduation."

"Hey, enough of that negative nonsense," chided Satin. "Nobody here is going to prison. Do I need to remind you yet again, one for all and all for one? The three musketeers, right?"

Goldie smiled feebly as they walked to their cars. *What a difference a day makes. Such a high for us yesterday, when we were all so euphoric. Such a low today. How in the world did this happen?*

Ruby unlocked her car door and climbed in. *Please God, I hope Goldie has no drugs in her house and that Satin can keep her occupied until the craving goes away.*

Satin adjusted the passenger seat in Goldie's car and stretched out her legs. *Looks like I might have to use my ace in the hole, after all. I hope it won't be necessary. Gotta do whatever it takes, though. Can't let Goldie be sent to the slammer. God, they could come after us as co-conspirators.*

CHAPTER 32

R uby took her place on the witness stand and smiled wanly at Goldie. She was ready to do her best to help obtain a "not guilty" verdict for her friend.

She cast her eyes along the members of the jury and was stunned when she recognized one of them. *How in the world did Shane get to be on this jury of all juries?* Her mind went back to when they first met at the fundraiser for the homeless several months earlier, and how much time they had spent together finding him a house in Las Vegas after his move from Oregon. *He looks as dashing as ever. Still so distinguished-looking with all that silver, wavy hair.*

Upon recognizing Ruby, Shane looked equally as shocked. He shifted uncomfortably in his chair, straightened his jacket, and tried to look away from her.

Ruby's mind swirled with the possibilities this chance encounter might have on the outcome of the trial, so much so that she did not hear the first question from the defense attorney. She suddenly snapped back to reality. "I'm sorry. Could you please repeat the question?"

"Would you tell the court your movements on the Fourth of July last year?"

Ruby provided a detailed explanation of the day, starting from the beginning, when Goldie picked her up and drove her to Satin's for the barbecue. With her words, she painted a picture of Satin's garden based on the tour they took. Looking back and forth at the jury, she said, "I remember making the fruit salad in the kitchen. Tchaikovsky's 1812 Overture was blaring so loud from the TV in the other room, I had to go outside and stoke the barbecue to escape the noise. We enjoyed the food on the patio. Then, the defendant took me home. Would have been about ten o'clock at night."

"So, you and my client were there all afternoon and late into the evening?"

"Correct."

"At no time did you or my client leave the house?"

"How could I? I didn't have my car. And I believe the neighbors, who seemed overly preoccupied with our feast that day, can attest that your client's car was parked outside the house the entire time."

"Was there anyone else at the barbecue?"

"No. Just the three of us. The neighbors were invited, but they didn't join us. They stayed on their porch. As I recall, your client actually took them a piece of the delicious cake I brought."

"I have no more questions for this witness."

"That was brief," Goldie whispered in his ear.

"No reason to belabor the point. She provided the perfect alibi. I can always re-direct, if necessary. Now hush, so we can hear what Madge has to say."

The prosecuting attorney strode toward the witness stand. "After consuming drinks on the patio, approximately how long were you inside, Ms. Smallwell?"

Ruby shrugged. "I don't know. A good couple of hours, I guess."

"Isn't that a long time to be preparing a fruit salad?"

Ruby was irked by the sarcastic question. "It was more than just a fruit salad. I chopped all the fruit, and while I was doing that, Gloriana was making the potato salad. When we were done, we decided to stay inside for a bit. It was a hot afternoon, so we watched some of the concert while soaking up the air conditioning. When we started to get hungry, Serena got the grill going and set the table while Gloriana and I cooked the meat."

"It didn't seem too hot for Ms. Young's neighbors."

Ruby answered drily. "Well, you would have to ask them how they felt. I didn't go to Serena's on the Fourth of July to discuss the weather conditions with her neighbors."

Madge looked at the Judge, who admonished the witness.

"Please, Ms. Smallwell, just answer the questions."

"Thank you, Your Honor," Madge continued. "Ms. Smallwell, I understand you have two young daughters. Where were they?"

"They were at my sister's."

"Do you normally spend the holidays apart?"

Brett objected, but he was overruled by the judge.

Ruby resented the injection of her girls into the trial. "As it happens, I'm happy to answer that question. My sister has a party every year on the Fourth of July. They really go all out — food, music, and fireworks. When my girls were really little, the fireworks scared them. So this year, I made plans for the three of us to go to Serena's party instead. But when I told the girls, they were sad. Since I already accepted the invite to the barbecue, I didn't want to back out. So, I just decided to let the girls go without me, so they could play with the cousins and spend some time with their aunt and uncle."

"How did the girls get to your sister's house?"

"I drove them there."

"You never mentioned that when the defense attorney asked you to recap the events of the day."

Ruby knew the prosecution was trying to trip her up. She smiled. "That's because I dropped them off the night before."

"And you didn't mention that you picked them up that night, either."

"That's because I picked them up the following morning."

"So you spent two nights away from your girls?"

Brett was on his feet. "Objection, Your Honor. Relevance? The witness isn't on trial here. The prosecution is on a fishing expedition."

The judge concurred. "I would agree. Move on, Ms. Williams."

"I have just one more question for this witness, Your Honor. What is the make and color of your car, Ms. Smallwell?"

Ruby crossed her legs. "I drive a red Audi."

"Thank you. I have no further questions." Madge returned to her seat

The judge banged his gavel. "The witness is excused. The court will stand in recess until two o'clock this afternoon."

Perfect timing, thought Ruby, as she headed out the courtroom. Satin was sitting in the reception area, reading a magazine. Ruby stopped next to her and made like she was fumbling for her car keys.

"Wig meeting in the ladies room in a couple of minutes," she whispered. "Urgent."

Satin waited a short while before following Ruby, who was busy powdering her nose. Satin stooped down and looked under the stalls before going into one and closing the door.

"Don't worry, I've already checked. Nobody's around," said Ruby. "Listen, we don't have much time. We'll be dead if we're caught. If you hear me cough, it means someone has come in, OK? I'll leave straight away, and you can come out a few minutes later. You've got plenty of time before you'll be called. Court's in recess until two o'clock. I think we've just scored a huge break. I know one of the jurors. He's a guy I met way back when at that ritzy fundraiser for the homeless we all went to. I think I told you about him — twice divorced from Oregon. His name is Shane. You know, the one who asked me to help him find a house. Obviously, unless he's moved, which I doubt, I know where he lives.

I'm going there after court finishes today, and I'll wait for him to come home. I'm sure I can talk him into voting 'not guilty.'"

"Wow! You're right, that is a lucky break. We sure could use it. How can you be sure he'll agree?"

"Oh, he'll agree. I'll just use the ruby-red charm. My testimony went well this morning. I'm sure yours will go equally as well this afternoon. I just need to see Shane face to face to seal the deal. I'm sure he'll believe my testimony and my alibi for Goldie. Incidentally, if the battle-axe, as you call her, brings up my kids, tell her you invited them to your barbecue, and I agreed, but then decided to send them to my sister's."

"Why would Madge ask me about your kids?"

"No time to explain. I'll join you and Goldie at the restaurant. Naturally, I'll be late. By the way, how was Goldie? She looked pretty pale from my viewpoint on the stand this morning."

"She was hellish last night. Very despondent. It was tough work trying to keep her spirits up. We talked for most of the night. I think her mood was a bit better this morning."

Ruby coughed loudly and grabbed a tissue from the box on the sink. She smiled to the lady who entered the restroom and left.

Satin waited a few minutes, exited the stall, washed her hands, and returned to the waiting area. *God, I hope Ruby's right and her Shane guy can pull us out of this.*

CHAPTER 33

atin avoided making eye contact with Judge Cavishaw as she stepped down from the witness stand. She headed toward the exit, heaving a sigh of relief when she heard Brett Lamont. "The defense rests, Your Honor."

The judge banged the gavel. "Very well. We stand adjourned until tomorrow morning at nine o'clock, when I will hear the closing arguments. A reminder to the jury not to discuss the case with anyone."

Satin drove to the French restaurant they had chosen for dinner that evening and reflected on the afternoon's events. *I don't think I'll ever forget Richard's face when I walked into the courtroom. I was probably the last person he expected to see. Looked like he'd seen a ghost. Serves him right for hanging up on me the last time we spoke. I would have told him I was the defense witness listed as Serena Young. And yikes, Goldie's right about Madge Williams. She's something else. I couldn't believe she'd ask if I'd received any phone calls that day. What an unwitting slip-up.* Satin chuckled out loud. *Nice break to be able to tell her I received only one call that evening, just as the TV concert was ending. Probably almost gave Richard a heart attack. He had to know I was talking about him, as he must have remembered calling me. Poor guy probably went apoplectic when I said I would provide the name and phone number.*

She removed one of her hands from the steering wheel and ran it loosely through her hair. *I knew the battle-axe would not want to continue that line of questioning or require me to provide the phone number. It wouldn't have helped her case. Must confess, I'm surprised though, Brett didn't call Goldie to the stand. Wonder what his rationale was.* She arrived at La Brasserie Exceptionelle, their designated dining spot for the evening, and waited in the reception area for Goldie. She didn't have long to wait.

"Where's Ruby?" Goldie asked as soon as she entered the restaurant.

Satin winked. "Let's grab a table first," she said. "We have some encouraging news."

The hostess led them to a quiet table in the corner, and they ordered their drinks.

"I had a brief talk with Ruby between our testimonies. She knows one of the jurors. She met him the night of that fundraising event we all attended. He'd just moved here from out of state somewhere. Anyway, I guess she helped him find a house. She says she can use her charm to call in a favor. She's going to join us later."

"That *is* good news. If anyone can ooze charm when they want to, it's Ruby, that's for sure. And hey, I certainly could use some good news after today."

Satin was taken aback. "What do you mean? I'm offended. I thought I was pretty good on the stand."

Goldie patted Satin's arms. "Oh, I'm not referring to you. You were fantastic. You didn't let Madge get to you at all. You were perfectly calm, despite the way she kept trying to trip you up. I was referring to our very own Perry Mason. Last night, he said it was our turn and to show confidence in him. He didn't do squat. His questions to you and Ruby were short, and you were then thrown to the mercy of the battle-axe."

"I think I did just fine, and I'm sure Ruby acquitted herself well. What was there for Brett to ask? He probably just wanted to make it short, since all he needs to do is provide evidence from more than one witness as to your whereabouts. I bet he'll be superb in his summation."

"You'd better be right," said Goldie. "Great, here come our drinks."

*****

On the other side of town, Ruby parked her car across the road from Shane's house, a few homes down and away from the streetlight. Even though it was almost dark, she put on her sunglasses and wrapped a scarf over her head. She was amused watching the young children play in the front yard next to Shane's. As much as she wanted a cigarette, she decided against it, not wishing to draw attention to herself. It wasn't long before she saw the door to Shane's garage opening and his car disappear inside. She checked her face in the mirror, played momentarily with the hair protruding from the scarf, grabbed her purse, headed toward the house, and rang the doorbell.

Shane was shocked when he opened the door. "What the hell are you doing here?" he yelled.

"Well, aren't you going to invite me in for a drink?" she asked in a demure tone.

Shane quickly looked around outside. Other than the kids laughing and kicking the football around, he saw no adults. He pulled Ruby into the living room and closed the door behind him. "Are you crazy, Ruby — or Rhonda — whatever your name is? This is highly irregular and inappropriate."

Very masculine, very Shane, she thought as she looked around the sparsely decorated home. "You have nice furnishings here, Shane. I'm impressed."

"You know, I should throw you out of here right now," he retorted, his voice getting angrier.

Ruby sat down on the Naugahyde sofa and removed her scarf and glasses. "But you won't," she said, lighting a cigarette. "I only came to make sure that you know my friend is innocent of the crime charged."

"The hell she is. She's as guilty as sin." Shane was pacing the living room, his hands in his pockets.

Ruby crossed her legs and adjusted her skirt. "The hell she's not. You heard my testimony today."

"I can't believe you're involved in this. Boy, did I misjudge you. That Dr. Priestly said it all. Gloriana whatever-her-name is confessed. That told me all I need to know."

"You can't take that into account. You know that."

"Hard to ignore when it comes from such an expert. I was with the jury when all hell broke loose. I heard the muttered comments from many of them. Your friend is doomed."

"Then you'll just have to be the naysayer. Didn't my testimony mean anything to you at all? We were with her the whole time, damn it!"

"Look, Ruby. I may not be a saint, but I sure believe in the rule of law. Your friend committed murder, no matter what cock-and-bull story you all concocted. She deserves whatever punishment is handed down to her." He placed his hands on the back of the couch and looked at her earnestly. "She took a man's life. A man is dead because of her. Doesn't that mean anything to you?"

Ruby extinguished her cigarette, and rose to face him. "If you really believe in the rule of law, then why aren't you ignoring the testimony of that counselor, as you were instructed by the judge?"

Shane headed toward the door and opened it. "You have your opinions of justice, and I have mine. Murder is murder. You may be able to condone it, but I can't. Nobody has a right to take someone else's life. The man she killed had hopes and dreams. He must have had family and friends who are mourning his loss. Now, I'm asking you to please leave."

What a sanctimonious creep, she thought, as she walked to the door. "I repeat, if you really believe in the rule of law, since you know one of the witnesses, you should at least recuse yourself. Which begs the question, why haven't you done that already?"

"Perhaps I should. Maybe I should also tell the judge that you've been tampering with the jury."

"Go ahead and do that, Sweetie. That will guarantee my friend a mistrial, even if she deserves to be acquitted." Ruby smiled and winked before she headed toward her car.

*****

"So, how did it go?" Satin asked as soon as Ruby sat down at the restaurant.

"Not as well as I'd hoped. Guess the old Ruby charm is beginning to fade. Goldie, he thinks you're guilty. He's one of those self-righteous rule-of-law creeps."

"Well, what was the upshot?" Satin beckoned the waiter.

"Tomorrow he says he's going to recuse himself because of jury tampering. The good news is, that will give us a mistrial. Of course, that presupposes he follows through and actually does recuse himself."

Satin stood up. "No, it doesn't guarantee a mistrial, Ruby. It guarantees that he'll be replaced with an alternate juror. Besides, we don't want a mistrial — Goldie needs an acquittal. That way, thanks to double jeopardy, she'll be free forever. You girls go ahead and have dinner without me. Time for me to play my trump card. I'll see you in court tomorrow." She left.

"What's her trump card?" asked Goldie.

Ruby shrugged. "Beats me."

Once in the car, Satin grabbed her cellphone from her purse and dialed a number. "I have some urgent information we need to discuss," she said as soon as she heard the voice on the other end. "I'll meet you at the Las Vegas Chinatown

Plaza at Spring Mountain and Arville in 15 minutes. Do you know where I'm talking about?"

"Yes, I know where it is. How urgent is this?"

"Urgent enough that we can't wait until tomorrow. When you enter the plaza, head straight to the Journey of the West Statue, and make a right. I'll park as close as I can to the Great Wall bookstore and the travel agency. I drive a white Jaguar convertible. The passenger side door will be unlocked. When you see me pull up, jump in."

"Why so clandestine and obscure?"

"It's only about a mile or so west of the Strip, off the street with a lot of foot traffic. We'll not be recognized. I'll see you in 15 minutes."

She hung up the phone and sped away.

CHAPTER 34

"God Almighty! That's one hell of a bombshell you've just dropped. I can't believe it."

Satin put her car into reverse and pulled out of the parking lot.

"Where are we going?" Brett asked.

"Nowhere in particular," Satin replied. "I just thought it might be easier to drive around the side streets as we talk, to make sure we won't be seen. Important thing is, am I covered with this information under the attorney-client privilege? And does it guarantee my friend an acquittal?"

"No, you're not covered by attorney-client privilege; I'll have to disclose it to Judge Cavishaw. Furthermore, he'll never grant an acquittal. The best we can hope for is a mistrial; however, he might instruct me to reveal the source."

"In which case, wouldn't it be better to ask for the case to be reopened, so you can put Goldie — sorry, I mean Gloriana — on the witness stand?"

"I would use that to force the Judge's hand, as well as the prosecution's, but I doubt they'll go for it."

"Look, the three of us can all attest to Goldie's relationship with Harvey. She met him at a fundraiser last year which we all attended. Harvey and Goldie were dancing the entire evening. He's quite flamboyant and definitely unmistakable, especially on the dance floor. Goldie saw him frequently after that night. He was one of the people who supported her coke habit. Quite often, it was in lieu of cash payment for her services."

"How did you piece all of this together?"

Satin lit a cigarette and lowered her window a little, so the air could circulate. "As you can imagine, in our business, we meet people from all walks of life and covering all professions. I'm not exactly computer literate outside of the system we use for our business, but I knew enough to search for Madge Williams. How was I to know she operates under her maiden name? I reached out to a friend of mine who has access to marriage licenses issued in Las Vegas and presto, up pops Harvey's name as her husband. Not only that, apparently Madge Williams has made her career out of convicting drug dealers and addicts, and here her husband is not only having a relationship with your client, but is supplying her drugs. Sounds to me like Madge is operating out of revenge, doesn't it? I mean, let's face it, her case has been flimsy at best."

"I can't imagine Madge knowing anything about this. She'd be mortified if she thought her husband was unfaithful. If Harvey has been paying Gloriana for her services, with prostitution being illegal in Vegas, he could face jail time. I've known Madge a long time. Revenge isn't her style."

"I'm not sure about that. Hell hath no fury like a woman scored, as they say. Maybe she knows and doesn't want to bring her husband in at this stage, because of the accusation of revenge. Maybe she'll go after him once she gets a conviction on Goldie. But whether Madge knows or not is irrelevant. Goldie will not go to jail. As you've stated, you have to share this information with the judge and prosecution," she said, turning yet another corner. It started to rain, so she switched on the windshield wipers.

Brett scratched his brow. "My head is just spinning. Can we go back to the parking lot? In light of this information, I've got my work cut out for me tonight when I get home.

But just for my own edifice, how long have you known about this?"

Satin turned the car into the opposite direction at the next set of traffic signals. "Since Madge Williams was assigned to the case."

"You do know I can nail you for obstruction of justice, don't you?"

"But you won't. You and I know that if this leaks out, all hell will break loose and there'll be such a scandal. I withheld information because I was hoping not to have to use it. Since I'm unsure of the outcome, I wanted you, the judge, and Madge to be aware. If an acquittal is out of the question, you and I both know the only option is a mistrial. You get me that, and I'll make sure the case never resurfaces."

"I still think that after my closing, the jury will acquit her anyway. Their case is, as you put it, flimsy at best."

They pulled back into the parking lot of the Chinatown Plaza. She switched off the engine. Brett stared straight ahead, looking at the neon lights flashing in the storefront windows as they listened to the sound of the rain falling on the windshield. Satin looked at him. "Believe me, the jury will probably find her guilty. They can't ignore the testimony of that broad from the rehab center."

"My God, you haven't been tampering with the jury, have you?" Brett looked at her astonished. He was still reeling from the earlier revelations, and now this?

"You really don't want me to answer that question, do you? As I said, our business puts us in touch with people throughout every corner of the community."

"I must say — it's a very, very clever plan you've put together. Who else knows about this information?" Brett asked, after a lengthy pause.

"At this point, as it pertains to the grounds for mistrial, just you and I know. Hopefully, by tomorrow, it will be the four of us, if you tell the judge and Madge."

"You mean neither of the other two ladies know?"

"Nope. And I don't intend to tell them, either. I think the least said, the better. After all, the name of our agency is Discreetly Yours." She turned and smiled at him. "As soon as this is over, I had planned on deleting your personal information from our records … as our way of saying thank you."

Brett heaved a sigh of relief. "I appreciate that. I hesitate to ask you this question, but I'm going to, anyway. Was there some behind-the-scenes plan to get Judge Cavishaw assigned to this trial?"

Satin smiled at him again. "Brett, I believe you said you have your work cut out for you this evening when you get home. It's getting late now. We need you to be fresh for court tomorrow. Don't you think you should get going? Where's your car? I don't want you to get wet."

She drove as close to his car as possible. "See you tomorrow."

He got out the car and ran quickly to his own vehicle. Satin watched him drive away. She texted Goldie and Ruby. "I believe we're all good. Until *mañana*. Delete."

CHAPTER 35

"**I** feel sick to my stomach," Goldie said, as she waited outside the courthouse with Satin and Ruby.

Satin put her arms around her friend. "You're going to be just fine, Sweetie. I promise you."

Ruby lit a cigarette. "I don't know how you can be so certain, Satin, or so calm. Even I'm feeling like a nervous wreck."

Satin glared at her. "I think it's time to go in." She ushered Goldie inside the courtroom. Annoyed that she had just sparked up, Ruby stomped out her cigarette butt and followed them.

"Ruby and I will be seated at the back, waiting — and rooting — for you."

They both gave Goldie a big hug, as she made her way to the front row. She sat next to Brett, and they both looked at the faces of the jury as they took their assigned seats.

"I'm ready to hear a Clarence Darrow closing, Perry Mason. I need something reassuring right now." Goldie was trying to make light of the situation. Before Brett could reply, Judge Cavishaw entered the room, and the bailiff called the court to order.

The judge was about to call for closing statements when Brett asked to approach the bench. "Some important information has come to my attention."

The expression on the judge's face reflected his annoyance. "Will both counselors please approach?"

Placing his hand over the microphone, he reprimanded the defense attorney. "I will not be amused if this is a fishing expedition."

"Your Honor, it might be better if we adjourned to your chambers. I believe the information I have is grounds for an acquittal." Brett knew an acquittal would not be forthcoming, but aimed for the optimum.

"I'll see both of you in my chambers. Now!" the judge ordered, his voice full of rage. He released his hand from the microphone. "The court will stand in recess for 15 minutes." He banged the gavel and left the courtroom, followed by the counselors.

Goldie turned to look at Satin and Ruby. Satin smiled and winked at her. Ruby was looking for a reaction from Shane, who was leaning forward, hands clasped, looking downward. She wondered whether he had actually followed through with his confession.

Back in the chambers, the judge issued a warning. "This better be good, Lamont. If I find you're taking us down a rabbit hole, you will be disbarred."

"No rabbit hole, Your Honor." Brett turned and looked at his fellow counselor. "I hate to be the bearer of this news, Madge. How much you know of what I'm about to reveal, I'm not sure." He returned to look the judge in the eyes. "I'm asking for an acquittal, Your Honor. Madge Williams operates under her maiden name. It transpires that her husband had an affair with my client last year. Naturally, my client didn't —doesn't - know he is married to the prosecutor."

Madge jumped from her seat, her face turning bright red. "This is outrageous. Even you would not stoop this low, Brett. My Harvey would never have an affair. He is faithful — always has been. A woman knows these things. With your permission, Your Honor, I can get my cellphone from my attaché case. It's on my desk in the courtroom. I can call Harvey to verify."

The judge turned to Brett. "This is a very serious allegation. Can you back it up?"

"I can, Your Honor. Of course, her husband's going to deny it, but what I'm telling you is true. I really believe this case merits an acquittal."

The judge was stern. "That's not going to happen, Mr. Lamont."

"If the case is not dismissed, Your Honor, I request permission to reopen the defense and call my client to the stand. It is my belief she will provide dates, times, and locations of their trysts. I'm hoping not to do that. It also appears that Madge's husband was feeding my client's drug habit." He looked at Madge sympathetically. He could tell from the pained and devastated look on her face that she was totally unaware of her husband's infidelity.

"I'm not sure how it would look for you, Madge, since you've made an admirable career out of prosecuting drug addicts and peddlers. You've established quite a reputation for yourself. Unfortunately, you haven't heard the worst of it. Your husband actually paid for my client's services. As you know, while escorts are legal in Las Vegas, prostitution isn't. Anyone paying for those services could face fines, a criminal record, and jail time, if convicted."

Madge sat down. Her face was white, tears streaming down her face.

The judge shifted uncomfortably in his seat. "Do you have any thoughts you care to share, Madge?" he asked, after a momentary pause.

She shook her head. "Right now, I am feeling numb and quite nauseated. Actually, I think I'm going to be sick. Please excuse me." She quickly rose from her seat and hurried from the chambers.

"How long have you known about this, Brett? It's quite a line to lay on the court at this stage of the proceedings."

"I recognize that, Your Honor. I found out last night after I closed for the defense. I swear, I truly believe my client is unaware she had been having a relationship with Madge's husband. I feel bad for Madge, but I have a duty to my client and to protect the integrity of the judiciary."

The judge looked askance. "Oh please, Brett, spare me that altruistic nonsense. It doesn't become you."

Brett moved his chair a little closer to the desk. "Look, Your Honor, if I open this up for my client to testify, who knows where it may lead? Once the press gets the story, who can say what might happen? It could be a huge scandal. Besides, Madge would be totally humiliated. Her career would be ruined." Brett was concerned for his own well-being, but the observation was not lost on Judge Cavishaw.

They looked at each other, both wondering whether the individual seated across the table was involved in any way. Both thought better than to pursue.

The judge tapped his fingers continuously on the desk. "I was not aware you were that fond of Ms. Williams, especially given your sparring in the courtroom during this trial."

"Doesn't mean I don't respect her. She's a formidable opponent. But she's good at what she does."

Madge returned to the room. "My apologies to you both for that. I hope you can understand my state of shock." She looked directly at Brett. "Do you know when this alleged affair started?"

"I believe it was last year, at a fundraiser for the homeless when they first met."

Madge nodded. "I remember it. I was visiting my sick mother at that time. Harvey went without me. Personally, I don't approve of an acquittal or a mistrial. I really believe she's guilty of the crime with which she's charged. In my opinion, I think the tramp should rot in hell. That said, I'm not sure what would be gained by dragging my husband's name, as well as mine, through the mud — even though my gut tells me he should go to jail, too. Naturally, I would have to disqualify myself. No matter what you decide, Your Honor, it will be a travesty of justice. However, I will accept your decision. Right now, my own judgement is not as it should be."

"I agree with Madge, Your Honor, insofar as accepting your decision. Naturally, I believe my client is innocent, and all the evidence from the prosecution has been weak. But if you do decide to proceed, I request a continuance. I think this would also be fair to the replacement of the prosecution, whoever that may be."

The judge thought for a minute, and then looked at both of them. "I'm fully aware that if I grant a mistrial, the case can be reopened by the office of the DA or the chief district attorney himself. I'm also concerned about the timing of this information being handed to you, Mr. Lamont. Who else knows about this?"

"Just the three of us, Your Honor, plus the individual who told me. Even my client is unaware, and I think we should keep it that way."

The judge looked straight ahead and could see the irony of his position as he absorbed the significance of the picture of Lady Justice on the wall facing him — her eyes blindfolded, holding the scales of justice in one hand, the sword in the other. "Will you both please leave my chambers and return to the courtroom? I'll meet you there shortly. I need to research for case precedent, to the extent there is one, and also consult with my fellow judges. Don't worry, Madge, I'll be discreet. Neither your name nor your husband's will be raised in my discussions."

As they returned to the courtroom, Madge confided to Brett. "When I go in, it will take all I can muster to refrain from punching your client out."

He grabbed her by the arm. "Madge, I'm truly sorry the way this has played out. I also feel bad about what this may have done to your marriage. I really hope the judge sees fit to grant a mistrial. That way, no one will ever know — nor will they need to."

Madge nodded. They entered the courtroom, to the sound of much chatter, and sat at their respective tables.

"What in the world is going on?" asked Goldie, both frightened and mystified.

"We'll have to wait and see. The judge will give us a ruling as to how he intends to proceed shortly. In the meantime, we wait." Brett started tapping his pencil on the desk again.

Goldie turned to Satin and Ruby and shrugged, raising her hands in the air. It was not too long of a wait before the judge reentered and made his way to the bench. The bailiff silenced the crowd. "Order in the court," he said loudly, for the second time that day. "The court is now in session, the Honorable Judge Cavishaw presiding."

The judge banged his gavel on the bench. "Ladies and Gentleman of the jury, this trial will be adjourned until three o' clock this afternoon. In the meantime, you're not to discuss this case with anyone, not least your fellow jurors."

Turning to the two counselors, he continued, "You'll arrive in court at the aforementioned time with your closing arguments prepared, even though there is a possibility they may be delayed in light of the discussion we just had. This court stands adjourned."

He banged the gavel and left the courtroom.

CHAPTER 36

I t was close to the moment of reckoning, and everyone reconvened in the courtroom.

"The last few hours have been total purgatory for me," said Goldie, as she sat beside her attorney. "I don't understand what is happening, or why you can't tell me what's going on."

Brett looked straight ahead as he tapped his fingers nervously on the table. "You know as much as I do. We just have to be patient and wait to hear what the judge has to say." She started to respond, but he motioned her to keep quiet.

At precisely 3.00 p.m., the bailiff called for order in the court and asked those present to rise. "The court is now in session," he boomed for the third time that day, "the Honorable Judge Richard Cavishaw presiding."

The judge entered the courtroom clutching a piece of paper in one hand and holding a pair of glasses in the other. Once he was in his chair, the bailiff instructed the courtroom to take their seats. There was a muffled sound as everyone scuffled with their chairs. Then, an immediate silence befell the entire room.

My God, you can hear a pin drop, thought Satin, who was seated next to Ruby at the back of the court. She tried unsuccessfully to make eye contact with the judge, who had a stern look on his face. *Maybe I've misplayed our hand.*

Meanwhile, Ruby was staring at Shane, who was still seated with his head down, his hands between his legs.

The judge scoured the room, looking first in the direction of the defense attorney and the defendant, then to the prosecutor, and finally to the crowd, observing Satin at the back of the room in the process. He picked up the piece of paper and donned his glasses. Assured of the attention of all present, he started to read, "Ladies and Gentleman, in the matter of the State of Nevada v. Berelowitz, I have recently been notified of some disturbing and troubling information that could potentially impact the accused's right to a fair trial. The scales of justice are sacrosanct. It is, therefore, with deep regret, that I have no alternative but to declare this case a mistrial."

He turned and faced the jury. "The court wishes to thank the jurors for their time and diligence in this matter. You are dismissed. Ms. Berelowitz, you are free to go," he said without turning to look at her. "This court stands adjourned." He removed his glasses, banged the gavel, and left the courtroom.

Goldie was stunned. "What happened? What does this mean?"

Brett rose. "Congratulations! Like the judge said, you are free to go."

"But I don't understand. Why? What caused it?"

"Don't worry about the whys and wherefores. You're free. The trial's over. That's all that counts."

She threw her arms around him, and tears started to roll down her cheeks. "Thank you, thank you, thank you."

He felt a little uncomfortable as he saw Madge looking at him, shaking her head.

"I think your friends are waiting for you at the back of the courtroom," he said, gently pushing his client away.

"Of course," Goldie replied, letting go of him. "I'll never forget what you did for me." She saw Satin and Ruby at the back hugging each other, and ran to join them."

Madge strolled over to Brett's table, briefcase in hand. "Too bad you didn't get to hear my closing. I would have creamed you," she said.

I doubt that, Brett thought. *I think I would have wiped the floor with your feeble case.* But given what she was going through, he decided to let it go. "I'm sorry for what this case has done to you, Madge. You know I had no alternative but to go to the judge."

She nodded.

"What are you going to do now?" he asked.

She shrugged. "I'm going to take a trip away for a few days. Maybe somewhere in California like Monterey or Carmel. Be by myself and figure out whether to file for a divorce or go and see marriage counselor. I might consider moving to another state and setting up a private law practice."

"You don't need to move to another state to do that."

"I know." She smiled at him, as they shook hands. "Thank you, Brett," she said.

"I wish you nothing but good luck, Madge."

"I'm not sure whether the office of the district attorney will re-open this case. With Gordon Roscoe backing off his original testimony, and without the testimony of Dr. Priestly, it will be a tough case to make." They both understood the system. As she headed toward the exit of the courtroom, Madge ignored Satin, who was making her way to see Brett.

"Thank you, Perry Mason," she smiled while extending her hand. "We're having a little victory party at our office this evening, if you would like to attend."

Brett was taken aback. "Thank you, but I think that would be highly inappropriate. I would like you to keep your end of our bargain though."

"I understand, but I wanted to extend the invite anyway. As for the other, it's already taken care of. You're already obliterated from all our records. As I stated from the outset, our word is our bond. Goodbye, Mr. Lamont, and thank you."

She turned and walked back to where Ruby and Goldie were still hugging each other. Brett closed his briefcase. *That sure is one classy and gutsy dame. Can't help but admire her.*

"OK, fellow musketeers, just enough time to go back and change for the party," said Satin.

"What party? And where?" asked Goldie. "I'm certainly in the mood to celebrate. What's the occasion?"

Ruby jabbed Goldie on the shoulder. "You are. Satin and I have it all arranged — a catered affair at our office at five o'clock to celebrate your court victory. After the events of this morning, we knew you were going to get off. We called the caterers and did a global email to our crew. Naturally, we didn't tell them the cause of the party, since we didn't know for sure that's what we'd be celebrating." They all laughed and left the courtroom.

"I've gotta run," said Satin. "I have a couple of things to do before tonight."

As Ruby and Goldie exited the courthouse, they ran into Shane.

"Why, Shane, thank you for coming through for us." Ruby smiled at him.

Shane was angry. "I did nothing, I'm ashamed to say. I don't know what went on in there, or what you did or said for this total miscarriage of justice that has just taken place."

Ruby put her arms around Goldie, who was clearly confused. "That's precisely where you're wrong, Shane. Trust me, justice truly was served."

"Don't you ever, ever contact me again, you hear?" He shook his finger at her before striding across the street.

Goldie was in a daze. "What the hell was that all about?"

"Oh, never mind him. Let's go and get changed. I'm ready to celebrate."

Meanwhile, Satin was already on her way to her destination. She dialed Richard's number on her phone.

"God, *now* what is it you want from me?" he answered, his tone clipped and curt.

"Just meet me at the Barnes & Noble on Charleston in thirty minutes. Same section as before," she said and hung up. She was absolutely positive he would show up, and he didn't disappoint. As he stood next to her in the science-fiction section, she could feel the same electricity she had experienced months before in the very same spot. "I just wanted to thank you for everything, Richard," she said as she pretended to browse nonchalantly through a book.

"You dragged me all the way out here, to tell me that?" he responded, equally as disinterested in the book he was holding.

"No. I wanted to give you these in exchange for burying the documents in this case, so it never resurfaces. I know you have the power and the wherewithal to make it happen."

"Why should I do that?"

"It's the right thing to do, that's why." She reached into her purse and pulled out the two books that she had held in her safe. "These have your fingerprints all over them. I am returning them to you. You no longer have to be looking over your shoulder, wondering whether you would be dealing with something similar to Madge Williams."

"How do you know about that? Were you the informant who gave that information to Brett Lamont?"

"Don't ask questions if you don't want to hear the answer."

"Did you have anything to do with keeping this whole case silent from the press?"

"I'll give you the same answer as I gave you before."

She handed him the books. "This is goodbye, Richard. No more questions. No more answers." She turned to leave, but he grabbed her on the shoulder. They looked into each other's eyes.

"I think you owe me the answer to at least one question. Why didn't you tell me you were Serena Young, a witness in the trial?"

"I was going to, but the last time we spoke, you put the phone down on me."

He nodded. "Trust me. I'll make sure the records are buried, although I doubt the DA's office will re-open the case," he said.

"Thank you." She believed him.

"Maybe in another time, in another place?" His voice trailed off.

She bit her lip. "Maybe." She removed his hand from her shoulder, and left.

*****

Ruby and Goldie were greeting everyone, trying to keep the secret of Goldie's mistrial a secret until Satin arrived. Many feared a guilty verdict. Many wondered whether the agency would be closing its doors. No announcement was made until everyone arrived.

Finally, Satin tapped her champagne glass with her knife. The room fell quiet. "Thank you all for coming tonight at such short notice. Goldie has an important announcement to make," she said gesturing in Goldie's direction.

Goldie started to cry. "Damn it, I promised myself this would not happen." The room went quiet as everyone feared the worst. "First, I would like to thank you all for your support — both financial and moral. It has meant the world to me. Today, the verdict came in — and I am a free woman." She threw her arms outward.

There was immediate applause followed by shrieks of congratulations. Everyone stampeded toward Goldie, suffocating her with hugs.

Ruby grabbed one of the bottles of champagne from one of the waiters and began circulating the room, filling everyone's glass. "So, let's eat, drink and be merry," she yelled over the noisy crowd.

Satin tapped her glass again. "Order in the office," she laughed, mimicking the behavior in the courtroom. "It's Friday evening. We know this is the busiest night of the week. You are all free to leave for your appointments. And, as our way of saying thank you, anything you earn tonight and tomorrow will be 100 percent yours to keep."

There was another roar of approval until one of the guys yelled out, "Hey, wait a minute. Goldie, did you actually do it? I mean none of us would blame you if you did. Let's face it, Frankie was such a jerk."

Before Goldie could answer, Satin replied. "You should all know by now that the middle name of all of us here is 'innocence,' right?"

Everyone laughed.

Ruby turned on a CD, and the sound of Kool and the Gang's "Celebration" started to play. Many of the women kicked off their shoes, took to the middle of the room, and started to dance. They were joined by the few men in attendance.

By nine o'clock, the party had fizzled out, with everyone leaving for their appointments. The catering crew and bartenders had cleaned up the dirty plates with their half-finished canapes, removed the lipstick-stained glasses, and departed the building, leaving a few bottles of champagne behind.

Ruby and Goldie lay back on the couches with their feet up, sipping their champagne. Satin remained at her desk, swiveling gently in her chair.

"So, what was that ace-in-hole you referred to yesterday, Satin?" Goldie asked. "And where did you go last night?"

"Oh, for heaven's sake, let's not rehash the past. Let's look forward. What are you going to do, Ruby?" She hoped she'd deftly switched gears.

"You know, if it's OK with you guys, I'd like to take Maria and Gabby to Disneyland for a few days, if you can cover for me. I've been promising them a trip there for ages. I want to see if my sister Margaret can come, too. She's been a jewel, and she loves the Magic Kingdom. What about you, Goldie? What are you going to do?"

Goldie ran her fingers through her hair. "I think I'm going to pamper myself this weekend," she said. "Tomorrow, I'm going to treat myself to a massage, maybe a facial and a good old mani-pedi. Sunday, I plan to go shopping and treat myself to some new clothes. I think I should stick around, in case the office of the district attorney decides to press charges again. You know what I mean? It's not like I was acquitted, where the rule of double jeopardy applies."

"Forget it," Satin said. "Not going to happen. Guarantee it. I promise you, it's all taken care of. So, what are you going to do after your shopping binge?"

"Wow, that's a huge relief. Well, after my pampering, I'm going to research what it takes to start a rehab center as I said I would. I might even check into buying the one I was in. The first thing I'd do is fire both Wendy-the-witch, the director, and that vicious counselor. Would I get a load of satisfaction out of that? What about you, Satin? What are you going to do?"

"I'm going to take a friend up on his offer to accompany him on a safari in South Africa."

Noticing the shocked expressions on her friends' faces, she immediately set their minds at ease. "No, I will not be sleeping in tents or camping out or anything like that. We'll be staying in five-star resorts every step of the way. The trip in the brochure looks fantastic. I've always wanted to go to South Africa."

"And just where did you meet this friend?" Goldie asked.

"Actually, he used to be a client here. He owns a travel agency. I'd been toying with the idea of a trip, so I went to see him. Thought I'd support his agency, since he supported ours." She laughed, as she toyed with her glass of champagne.

"Methinks you're holding out on us, Satin," Goldie teased.

Ruby sat up. "Me too. Just how serious is this? Do I hear wedding bells, or is it just the sound of the wind chimes through the kitchen window?"

Satin lit a cigarette and laughed again. "Believe me, you two will be the first to know. We'll see how it goes on the trip. As you know, it has long been my dream to get married and settle down."

Ruby was surprised. "But, what does he think about your past, and about you running this agency?"

"As a matter of fact, he has no trouble with my running the agency, and he seems fine with my past … as long as it is in the past, and he doesn't have to pay."

They all laughed.

"Well, I hope it happens for you, Satin." Ruby raised her glass. "Here's to you and your dreams."

Satin picked up her glass, and went to join her friends. "And here's to yours, Goldie."

Goldie lifted her glass and filled it with more champagne. "And here's to you and your girls, Ruby. May they always bring you the happiness you deserve. Cheers."

They all clinked their glasses.

The phone rang.

Satin returned to her desk and answered in her usual demure tone, "Good evening. Discreetly Yours. How may I be of service?"

TO MY READERS

Thank you so much for reading this novel, which I hope gave you much pleasure.

If you enjoyed my book, I would be most grateful if you would consider submitting a review to any or all of the following:

- My website at www.discreetlyyours.net
- Amazon at www.amazon.com
- Goodreads at www.goodreads.com

For a complete list of other novels I have authored, please visit my author website at www.authorstephenmurray.com

Happy reading!

Stephen Murray
stephen@casandras.net